How the Lady Cha

How the Lady Charmed the Marquess

Laura A. Barnes

Laura A. Barnes

2020

First Printing: 2020
ISBN: 9798555947420
Laura A. Barnes
Website: www.lauraabarnes.com
Cover Art by Cheeky Covers
Editor: Polgarus Studios

To Icey & Lincoln,

Thank you for helping Mema name her characters.

I love you silly monsters!

Chapter One

Charlotte Holbrooke, Charlie to her family and friends, trudged along the walking path around the house, her slippers kicking at the gravel. She'd left her sisters and cousin in the library, poring over the latest fashion plates. Uncle Theodore's news during dinner had heightened their excitement. News in which Charlie found no pleasure. Why now? She didn't want to leave while Sapphire was due to give birth any day now. While she wouldn't be the one who delivered the foal, Charlie wanted to offer comfort to Sapphire during the birthing process. Who wanted to prance around like a lady trying to capture a gentleman's interest during the London season? Not her. Charlie found it unpleasant when Uncle Theo made her wear a dress during dinner.

She had followed Abigail out of the library, but lost sight of her in the darkness. Charlie understood why Abby left and wanted to ease her discomfort. Even though they were all wards of Uncle Theodore, because their fathers were his brothers, Abby wasn't. She had been the maid's daughter to her Aunt Paulina. When tragedy had struck Charlotte's family, killing her parents, aunts, uncles, and their servants in a boating accident, Abigail was left all alone. Uncle Theo took her under his wing and included her in their family. Since Abby came from a servant's family, the ton wouldn't accept her. Charlie's family considered Abigail as one of them, but others would not.

Raised voices bellowed out from the open window further along the path. Charlie gathered her skirts in one hand, stepped into the grass to muffle her footsteps, and made her way closer to the window. She pressed against the stone façade, listening to her cousin, Lucas Gray, arguing with Uncle Theodore. Only Uncle Theo wasn't so much arguing back, but laughing off Lucas's points on why allowing the girls a season in London all at once was madness.

"Are you quite mad, old man?" Lucas asked.

"On the contrary, I am quite sane."

"Well, I disagree. First thing tomorrow, I will consult with the lawyer on how to lock you up in Bedlam."

Uncle Theodore laughed. "Pour me one of those too, since you want to argue this out."

Charlie watched Lucas's reflection in the window while he poured them each of glass of whiskey. She noted Lucas filled his glass near the rim. Charlie wrinkled her nose, grimacing at the drink. She had tried it once before and didn't have a pleasurable experience with the toxic liquid. How they took enjoyment from it was beyond her.

"First off, dressing four females at one time for the London season will break the bank," Lucas replied wryly.

"We have plenty of money to spoil on these ladies and they deserve it. However, not four, but five."

Five? Charlie mouthed.

"Five?"

"Yes, you are forgetting Abigail."

"But she is not a lady, father. The best you could offer to Abigail is to present her as a lady's companion."

Charlie fumed. At times, Lucas could be an imbecile. Not a lady? Abigail acted more like a lady than Charlie. How dare he insult Abigail?

"I will pretend you did not utter those remarks concerning Abigail. We have raised her to be a lady, and so she is. I am ashamed of your blatant disregard for the girl."

Lucas sighed. "I meant no disrespect, Father. You know I do not consider Abigail as such. I only argue on how others will perceive her."

"Well, I have never cared for how others think, only for how I do. As should you, my boy. Now, let us hear your other arguments, and then I shall inform you of my plans."

"Never mind. I do not wish to insult my cousins, any more than I meant to insult Abigail. You know of their faults, and how others will judge them. If you believe they are ready, then I must accept your judgment. However, for the record, let it be known that I still think this is madness."

Uncle Theo laughed again. "Duly noted, my boy. Before the season begins, I thought we would host a house party. Introduce the girls to some gentlemen, so they can practice their flirtation skills. At the end of the party, we will throw a ball. This will also give them some practice on how to organize an event. They can help your Aunt Susanna with the planning."

Lucas shook his head in defeat. Charlie's ire at him grew. Obviously, he found fault with all of his cousins' qualities. While Uncle Theo was a relaxed man who went along with the mood, Lucas was a stickler for all things proper and planned. He never veered off course. Even down to accepting his fate of marriage. Uncle Theo had arranged a betrothal when Lucas was a lad. It was to the daughter of another prominent duke. Upon their marriage, as the only children of dukedoms, they would amass a substantial fortune. It was a shame that Uncle Theo didn't wait to see how the lady's character would shape. As it stood, her cousin would end up married to a shrew. Maybe after Lucas married his shrew, he would appreciate how amazing Abigail was. By then, it would be too late.

"Each girl will require a new wardrobe. Can we not introduce one lady at a time? Since Jacqueline is the oldest, why not let her have a season this year? The following year, the twins can have their chance, then the year after, Gemma and Abigail can make their debut." Lucas continued to reason with his father.

"All those seasons will not be necessary."

"Do you believe each lady will succeed in their first season?" Lucas scoffed.

Charlie growled. Lucas had gone too far. She wanted to step in front of the window and inform him so. But she wanted to listen to her uncle's response more. Charlie knew eavesdropping benefited no one. But if their season was part of a bigger plan, Charlie needed to learn as many details as necessary. Then she could inform the other ladies what was at stake.

"Have you heard anything interesting?" A voice whispered from behind her.

Charlie stilled, rolling her eyes. Another insufferable male with whom they were expected to share the evening. She had forgotten about Lord Jasper Sinclair. He had joined their family for dinner. Again. Charlie had gotten so lost in Uncle Theo and Lucas's conversation that she didn't notice Sinclair wasn't present and taking part in the lively discussion. She was positive Sinclair would have had his own opinion, if so.

Charlie turned and put a finger to her lips. "Shh." And turned back to listen.

"If they wanted you to listen, they would have invited you to join them," Sinclair whispered louder.

Charlie closed her eyes, gritting her teeth. If she couldn't get rid of Sinclair, then she risked Lucas discovering her. Charlie turned back, raised her hand, and gave Sinclair the motion to move on. However, she couldn't deter the marquess.

She tried, "This does not concern you, Sinclair."

"Ahh, then it must concern you. Perhaps, I wish to listen too, you know, just in case. Move aside, love. I am a bit curious myself."

Sinclair placed his hands on Charlotte's waist and lifted her effortlessly behind him. Charlie growled. The brute. He would get them caught with his high-handed ways. Sinclair looked over his shoulder and winked at Charlie. His smile was contagious. Charlie shook her head—Sinclair's smile was her downfall. No matter how much he infuriated Charlie, all he had to do was to flash that sparkling smile her way. And she melted. Literally melted. Melted into a simpering maid at his beck and call.

Jasper Sinclair sensed Charlotte was shooting daggers at his back. The smile would only halt her for so long before Charlotte would shove him to the side. She shouldn't be spying on her uncle and cousin anyway. However, Sinclair's curiosity had grown when Gray asked Sinclair to excuse himself after port. He'd wondered what Gray needed to discuss with his father so urgently. Sinclair thought it had something to do with the announcement the duke made at dinner. A very generous offer for the young ladies, who became excited and exclaimed with glee. Except for Charlotte and Abigail.

Sinclair understood why Abigail wouldn't find joy with the news. With her standing in society, Abigail wouldn't be able to attend most functions to which the other ladies would receive invitations. If she did, it would have to be as a companion, not as a lady seeking to draw the attention of a gentleman to court her. Sinclair had a few connections who would find pleasure in having Abigail Cason for a wife. Sinclair would follow up on them when they traveled to London and make the necessary introductions. He, like the other families in the county, held a soft spot for the miss.

He also understood why Charlotte would balk at the idea. Sinclair laughed to himself, knowing full well Charlie hated being in a dress at this very moment. He could only imagine her forced into silk and lace, acting all prim and proper. Sinclair's shoulders shook while he pictured the storm Charlie would create in the ton.

"What is so humorous, you buffoon?" Charlie hissed.

Her comment set him off. Sinclair let out a bark of laughter, drawing Gray's attention to the open window. When Gray drew closer, Sinclair shook his head and mouthed *Charlie* to him. Gray nodded and spoke louder.

"We should join the ladies in the library, Father. We can continue this discussion at a later time."

"Nothing more to discuss, my boy. My decision is final."

Sinclair waited until the duke and his son left the study before he turned around. Charlie's glare only made his smile grow wider. He loved provoking her into a tiff. Sinclair shrugged in apology.

"Sorry, nothing more to learn."

"Do you not have a home to return to?"

"Yes, my lady, I do. But I shall return here soon."

"Whatever for?"

"Your uncle has extended an invitation to his house party. I do not wish to miss it for the world."

Sinclair bowed and walked away towards the house before Charlie responded. He knew he left her irritated and took great pleasure from it. From what he overheard, it appeared the duke had a plan for the house party involving his wards. The duke meant to play matchmaker, and Sinclair wanted no part of it. However, it would be enjoyable to observe. He must steer clear of ever being alone with any of the ladies. Especially Charlotte. There was something about the chit attracting him to her. Probably just the amusement of her mischiefs. It had nothing to do with … no, of course not.

Charlie watched Sinclair round the corner of the house before she breathed again. She rested her hands on her waist. Her body still tingled from his touch. Why did the one gentleman who was so infuriating hold such an effect on her? Not only had Sinclair flustered her this evening, but he also prevented Charlie from learning what her uncle had planned for them. At least she learned some of his agenda. She would wait until tomorrow morning to share the information. For now, Charlie only wanted to savor Sinclair's touch a little while longer.

Chapter Two

Charlie slipped inside Abigail's bedroom, searching until she found Abby with her back to the room, staring out the window. Abby held a hot chocolate, taking small sips.

"Do you not agree, Abigail?" Gemma asked.

"Yes, dear." Abby glanced over her shoulder, bestowing Gemma with a smile.

Charlie noticed the sadness in Abigail's eyes. Would it change once Charlie shared her news? Or would Abigail see Uncle Theo's offer as charity? Even though it was anything but charity. Uncle Theo considered Abigail to be family, as they all did. Only Abigail always tried to maintain a distance, believing herself unworthy of their love. When Abigail's gaze landed on Charlie, she smiled wistfully.

"Good morning, Charlotte."

The rest of the girls offered their early morning greetings in between discussing the grand adventure they were about to embark on. Charlie needed to share with them the news. Then, Abigail would feel comfortable in her own bedroom.

Every morning the girls would meet for hot chocolate and pastries, discussing their plans for the day. The routine had begun after their arrival to live with Uncle Theo. All of them were out of sorts, and this early morning ritual gave them the stability they needed. They would crawl out of bed, pull on their dressing gowns, and invade a different bedroom every day. Today of all days happened to be Abigail's room.

"Is this not the most exciting news, Charlie?" Gemma gushed.

Gemma would be the most excited of them to enjoy a London season. She was the epitome of a perfect lady. She had followed all their lessons as taught, dressed fabulously, and her manners were impeccable. Gemma would capture many hearts throughout this ordeal. However, she should have been the most sensitive to Abigail. Especially since they were as close as sisters. Abigail's mother had been the maid to Gemma's mother. They had been the best of friends while their parents lived, and now they *were* sisters.

"Not really," Charlie muttered.

Gemma laughed. "You will change your opinion once we arrive in London. Our days will be filled with sights to see, shops to explore, and balls to attend. I am positive Uncle Theo will even take you to Tattersalls to help him purchase more horses for his stock."

Charlie hadn't thought of visiting London's premiere horsing establishment. Perhaps London didn't sound so terrible after all.

"Do you imagine so?"

"I am sure you could persuade him to," Charlie's older sister Jacqueline answered.

"That is, if we even make it to London," replied Charlie.

"Why would we not? Uncle Theo told us at dinner his intentions. Has he changed his mind? And how do you know?" Evelyn, her twin sister asked.

All eyes pinned Charlotte with questions. She didn't want to admit to this part. While they would appreciate what she'd learned, they would be upset with her for eavesdropping. Her unlady-like habit had gotten them into trouble many times. Even causing them to miss out on joining special events. The last time Charlie convinced them to snoop, they had lost out on attending the village fair. Charlie had persuaded the rest of the girls to spy on Lucas's picnic with his betrothed, Selina Pemberton. Uncle Theo had pressured Lucas to start his attempts to court the miss, even though their engagement was solid. Uncle Theo explained that even though they'd secured the girl's hand, she still deserved the courtly rituals. In Charlie's opinion, Selina didn't deserve the special treatment at all, or Lucas for that matter.

They had hidden themselves across the pond behind the bushes and watched Lucas's sorry attempt at courting. Not that the poor bloke hadn't tried, it was just that his fiancée didn't appreciate his charm. When Lucas had accidentally poured lemonade down Selina's dress, the spying girls started giggling. Luckily, Lucas hadn't heard them. In his clumsy attempt to help Selina clean her dress, Lucas bumped her into the pond. At his every attempt to pull her out, she only sunk deeper into the mud. The girls had started laughing harder.

When Charlie tried to peer over Gemma's shoulder, doubling over in laughter, she caused them to fall through the bushes. They exposed their hiding place, showing them having great delight in Lucas's predicament. It made for an interesting afternoon.

Before their appearance, Selina had been berating Lucas. Then when she had an audience, she turned on the waterworks. When Lucas managed to pull her out, Selina's maid rushed over with a blanket and helped her back to the house. Her wails grew louder the further she stormed away. Lucas glared at them, shaking his head while he gathered the picnic basket, and followed Selina. Once Selina reached the house, she cried her distress to her father and Uncle Theo. She blamed the girls' presence for her misfortune. Uncle Theo forced them to apologize to Selina and then punished them by forbidding them to attend the village fair. Selina had gloated throughout dinner, her calculated gaze assessing each girl with triumph.

"Um, I might have overheard Uncle Theo and Lucas on my walk outside after dinner." Charlie winced.

"They were holed up in Uncle's study after dinner. If you overheard anything, it meant you were eavesdropping again. Have you not learned your lesson?" Jacqueline reprimanded.

"It was not my intention. I was taking a walk along the path and their raised voices floated out the window. When I stopped to remove a pebble from my shoe, I overheard …"

"*Charlotte*," Evelyn said. "The truth. Do not make up stories."

Charlie sighed. The worst part of having a twin was that her sister always knew when she lied.

"All right. There was no pebble. But I only stopped because Lucas was shouting at Uncle Theo. I grew concerned. They were discussing Uncle Theo's promise to our debut into London society this year, so I decided to listen. In all fairness, it concerned us. I believe Uncle's offer is only a façade."

Each girl glanced at the other in question before returning their focus on Charlie. She saw their questions, but only had a few answers for them. The rest they would need to learn on their own. Between the five of them, they would have no trouble in discovering their uncle's agenda.

"What makes you think he plays us false?" asked Jacqueline.

"Well for starters, before we travel to London, he plans on hosting a house party where we can practice our social skills. Or in Uncle Theo's words, our flirtation skills." Charlie rolled her eyes.

"That sounds marvelous. Who does he plan to invite?" asked Gemma.

"He did not say."

"Charlie, if you are going to listen to other people's conversations, you need to learn to do a better job of it," Gemma scoffed.

"Well I learned …" Charlie began, watching Abigail sneak toward the door.

"What did you learn?" Evelyn asked.

"You may wish to stay, Abigail. This concerns you too."

Abigail paused with a hand on the doorknob. "I do not see how?"

"Why would it not?" Gemma asked Abigail.

Abigail sighed. "Gemma, I cannot be presented into society. I am not one of you."

"What nonsense. You are family."

Abigail smiled patiently, waiting for someone to explain to Gemma what she couldn't. She wouldn't embarrass Gemma with an explanation now. Abigail would explain later. When no one spoke, Abigail sat next to her friend on the bed and offered a hand. When Gemma clasped it, Abigail turned her attention to Charlie.

"Continue with your explanation, Charlotte," Abigail urged.

"Abigail, Uncle Theo's offer extends to you too. When Lucas objected to Uncle's plans for our entrance into society, he clarified that you would be included."

"Why would Lucas object?" asked Jacqueline.

"First, he mentioned the cost of financing a new wardrobe for each of us. Then he made a comment to what a disaster it would be, considering our personalities."

"What is wrong with our personalities?" asked Abigail.

"He did not go into detail. Then Uncle Theo implied that if his house party were a success, not all of us would have a London season. Why would he imply that?"

"Because it would appear our uncle plans on playing matchmaker. He plans on us making matches with his guests. The sneaky devil," said Jacqueline.

"Why would he offer each of us a chance at a London season, if he did not mean it?" asked Evelyn.

"Because he wishes to trick us into believing the house party was an introduction of what we would expect once we reach London. He plans on our excitement of entertaining his guests and throwing a ball, all the while manipulating us into marriages," Jacqueline explained.

They each sat, pondering the implications, helpless if that were the case, their doubts and insecurities rising to the surface. None of them had parents who would object for them. They were at the mercy of Uncle Theodore. Not that their uncle's actions were an act to relieve himself of their care. No, Uncle Theo's actions were of an old man who wanted his wards secured in the world before anything happened to himself. After his bout with pneumonia last year, he worried that their futures weren't settled. Yes, Lucas would see to their care, but not with the same heart Uncle Theo had. Uncle had spoiled them, catering to their every whim. While Lucas, once he married Selina, would still be generous toward their care, his wife would find a reason to remove each lady from the estate at the earliest convenience.

"This is even more splendid. Eligible bachelors at our beck and call. We will not have to compete with any other ladies. And Uncle Theo will only invite the very best," said Gemma.

Leave it to Gemma to find a positive outlook for this affair. Although outwardly reserved, she also looked on everything in life as a grand adventure. To her, every cloud had a silver lining.

"Gemma has a point. We should all approach this house party as a chance to step out of our comfort zone and indulge in a gentleman's attention. A little light flirtation will be great practice for when we take London by storm. When I mean a gentleman's attention, I am only implying conversation and nothing else. Do you understand? We will not put ourselves in situations that we cannot undo. Also, we will only consider marriage if it is a love match and nothing less. If it does not happen, then Uncle Theo will take us to London. Do we agree on this?" asked Jacqueline.

"Agreed." Every girl nodded except for Abigail. Charlie noticed Abigail still didn't believe Uncle Theo included her in his invitation. Or else she refused to take part. Either way, Charlie would make it a goal to find somebody worthwhile for Abigail to love. She had thought, at one time, that gentleman would be Lucas. However, with his betrothal he couldn't throw Selina to the side. After hearing Lucas's remarks from the previous evening about Abigail, Charlie realized she had been mistaken about her cousin's regard toward Abigail.

"Now, what else did you overhear?" asked Jacqueline.

"Yes, well, I was unable to hear the rest of the conversation. More like, someone interrupted me."

"Oh no. Did Lucas and Uncle Theo catch you?" asked Evelyn.

"No, not them," Charlie sighed.

"Then who?"

"Sinclair," Charlie growled.

A hush fell over the room. All eyes stared at Charlotte again. Each lady held a different meaning with their look. Not wanting to wonder what they might all suggest, Charlie rose from the chair and walked to the window. She knew Jacqueline's stare was one of a parental sort that implied at the inappropriate nature of Charlie being alone with Sinclair in the dark. The smirk from Gemma was one of envy. Every girl in the county wanted to be alone with the rake. Everyone except Charlie. Evelyn had tilted her head with a questioning stare. Charlie could explain away every look, but one. Evelyn's stare was the only one that made Charlie uneasy. There was too much truth in her twin's gaze. One that Charlie didn't want to analyze. To do so would open Charlie to emotions she didn't want to discuss with a soul, even with Evelyn.

"That overbearing man moved me out of the way, so he could listen himself. Then he refused to tell me what he overheard. He only laughed. And to make matters worse, Sinclair is one of the gentlemen Uncle Theo extended an invitation to. Now I will have to suffer through his annoying company for the next week. Why does he even need to stay here? His home is only a half-hour ride away."

"Perhaps he wishes to win your hand?" Gemma teased.

Charlie snarled.

"Or maybe mine," Gemma said wistfully.

Charlie shook her head at the foolishness. Every gentleman within a one-mile radius, Gemma sighed over. Jasper Sinclair was no exception. And Gemma was no exception to Jasper Sinclair. He always flirted shamelessly with her cousin. Gemma enjoyed the attention and flirted back. Was he joining the house party for a chance to win Gemma? The thought didn't sit well with Charlie. Not that she wanted him for herself.

"This is the exact behavior that must not happen when this house party is in full swing. I understand Uncle Theo has been lenient with our behavior over the years. However, we must not bring shame on our family. I know Sinclair is a regular staple in our lives. But during this time, we will all behave differently toward him. No more private moments with Jasper Sinclair. And that includes you too, Charlotte," Jacqueline ordered.

"I do *not* wish to be alone with that man," Charlie said.

While the rest of the ladies discussed their plans for the house party, Charlie reflected on the certain gentleman. *Did* she secretly wish to be alone with Jasper Sinclair? Did Charlie want Jasper to scandalously flirt with her too? Charlie touched her waist and remembered how his touch last night, but for a brief moment, had affected her. Did Sinclair wish to be alone with her?

Chapter Three

The bark of the oak dug into Charlie's arm. She wanted to sink into the lush green grass and lean against the tree, but that would only ruin the new day dress and send Aunt Susanna into a fit. She wasn't really her aunt, but all the girls addressed her as such. Aunt Susanna was Lucas's aunt, his mother's sister. When they had first come to live with Uncle Theo, she stayed for a while, helping everyone adjust to their new lives. Throughout the years, she had been a comfort, always holding her arms open to cry in, answering questions none of them wanted to address with Uncle Theodore, and offering advice. Aunt Susanna was the closest they had to a mother. Charlie didn't want to upset her, when Aunt Susanna had worked so hard to make the house party a success. Charlie knew they were searching for her right now, but she didn't want to leave this sanctuary. This old oak tree had been her salvation whenever she needed to gather her thoughts and build confidence.

Charlie tugged on the material, trying to raise the dress higher. The front of the dress, while demure and perfectly acceptable for a lady, displayed more skin than she usually preferred. When Charlotte had dressed along with Evelyn in their bedroom, the transformation was astounding. She had stood in front of the mirror regarding the miss staring back, while Polly dressed Evelyn's hair. Polly had given Charlotte a simple up-sweep with a few tendrils hanging loose. Now Charlotte's cheeks were flushed, and she appeared to be a beauty. Charlotte frowned.

A beauty, she scoffed. Who did she fool? Now, Evelyn, *she* was a beauty, and a natural-born lady. Charlie was unpredictable, no one ever knowing what fool thing she would attempt next, and there were the unrefined conversations. She questioned everything. In contrast, Evelyn was quiet, demure, polite, and very much predictable. They may have been identical in looks, but their personalities were at opposite ends.

Charlie watched the carriages arrive in the drive. Aunt Susanna and Uncle Theo greeted them, and Gemma, Abigail, and her sisters were waiting in the parlor to meet the guests. Where she should be at this moment, but Charlie couldn't bring herself to leave this one safe place where she could be herself.

Lucas stood correct. Uncle Theo was mad. Oh, Charlie knew his full intention for this house party. Did he expect they could charm the gentlemen he invited into offering for their hands? Especially her? The idea only made Charlie want to cringe. Even the house party was out of the norm. No one hosted house parties in the spring—the summer or early fall were the appropriate times. However, no one would speak otherwise against Uncle Theo, because of his eccentric ways. No one dared to cross the powerful duke. If he wanted to have a house party in the spring, then it would be the talk of the ton on what a grand notion it was. His peers probably tried any means to receive an invitation. Only to be disappointed, because Uncle Theo had already made his guest list and sent the invitations before gossip spread.

The pounding of horse hooves thundered closer. Charlie pressed closer to the tree, trying to hide behind the enormous trunk. Only one man would come from that direction. Perhaps he wouldn't notice her and continue on to the house. The one man she didn't wish to converse with, let alone see. Lord

Jasper Sinclair. The marquess whose property bordered Uncle Theo's. The same gentleman who infuriated Charlie, then in the next minute left her in a muddled state of confusion. Sinclair could provoke her into outlandish acts, then seduce Charlotte with a calming voice like he had done the evening outside the study. Yes, the last gentleman she wished to deal with.

"Hiding again, are we?" asked Sinclair.

Charlie closed her eyes and started counting to ten. Once she reached ten, she continued to count. There wasn't a number high enough that would ever give her the patience to deal with Sinclair. With a deep breath Charlie opened her eyes and addressed him with polite indifference.

"No, Lord Sinclair. I am only taking a breath of fresh air before welcoming Uncle Theo's guests."

"Lord Sinclair? I quite like the sound of that from your lips," he whispered, brushing a stray curl from her cheek.

Charlotte tried to back away from his touch, but only pressed closer to the tree. She narrowed her eyes at his cryptic reply. What did he imply? He arched his eyebrows and smiled his devilish charming smile. Sinclair laid his palm above her head and leaned in closer. Charlie didn't trust the look in his eyes and darted under his arm, putting much needed distance between them. Why was he toying with her? The insufferable brute. She needed to control her temper. She had made a promise to Jacqueline and Aunt Susanna that she would act like a proper lady this week. Charlie wouldn't ruin the other girl's chances at finding a suitable mate. She had no intention of falling for Uncle Theo's matchmaking, but she wouldn't be the reason if *they* didn't find their true love.

Jasper chuckled to himself. He enjoyed teasing Charlotte Holbrooke. In the past, he teased her to get a rise out of her temper and to provoke Charlotte into taking a dare. Every single time she would try to prove Jasper wrong. Sometimes she did—and then there were other incidents that landed Charlotte in trouble. He took much pleasure from those. Lately, his teasing had turned into more of a flirtation. He held no intention of taking it any further, but when her cheeks flushed pink as they did now and she became flustered, not knowing how to respond, Jasper's fascination grew. His scandalous remarks confused the innocent miss. Jasper wondered how Charlie would react if he ever took them further. Would she sigh against his lips, or would she rain on him with a tirade that blistered his ears?

Once Charlie escaped under his arm, he leaned against the tree, crossing his ankles. While she nuzzled his horse, whispering to the stallion, he noticed her unsettled state. Poor Charlotte. Her uncle's machinations made her vulnerable. A characteristic very becoming on her, even though Charlie would disagree. He decided to take pity.

"Are you nervous?" he asked.

Charlie glared at him. "Of course not."

So she wanted to act defensive with him. Jasper wouldn't react to her ire. Instead, he continued his flirtation. He saw the effect of his charm on Charlie and wanted to see more blushes.

"You look lovely today."

Charlie felt her cheeks grow warm. She couldn't blame it on the weather, because the sun hid behind the clouds. Charlie knew it was from Jasper's voice deepening while he complimented her. She should thank him for the compliment, but felt herself falling into that muddled state.

"May I offer some advice on how to survive this ordeal?"

"How?" Charlie asked before she could stop herself.

"I can be your confidant, if any of the gentlemen piques your interest, and if you wish for them to pursue you. I can advise you on how to win them over and offer my opinion on their character."

"Why would you offer to do this?"

Jasper shrugged. "Because I do not agree with your uncle's plan. You will be out of your elements with the gentlemen in attendance. They can be a predatory sort."

Charlie lifted her chin and pushed her shoulders back.

"I can handle any gentleman Uncle Theo has invited."

Jasper groaned at the sight of an agitated Charlie with her breasts pressing tight against the gown. A gown that plunged lower than the usual dresses she wore. Was he the mad one proposing his assistance on finding Charlie a match? He took a step closer, still keeping a respectable distance between them. However, Charlie retreated a step anyway.

"I agree, my dear. I am only implying they are jaded and might corner you in an inappropriate situation. There are ways you can tempt them while still keeping your innocence, and I am willing to teach you how."

"But if I tempt them, will they not try even more to corner me?"

"Not if you imply certain aspects to your temptation."

"What if I choose not to entice these gentlemen? What if my only goal is to fool my uncle into believing I attempted to find myself a husband?"

Again, Jasper took a few steps forward. Only this time Charlie remained planted in the same spot. His intense gaze kept her from moving.

"Is that your intention?" Jasper asked.

"Yes," Charlie whispered.

"Perhaps we can strike a deal then?"

"And what might that be?"

"I can pretend an interest in you in return for a favor."

"What favor might that be?"

"If we can convince your uncle that I am smitten with you, then you will convince him to sell me Sapphire's offspring."

"No," Charlie snapped.

"Then I shall leave you at the mercy of the attending gentlemen."

Jasper gathered the reins to his horse, ready to finish the ride to the Colebourne estate. He dangled the offer, knowing that Charlie wouldn't agree right away. She would stew over his proposal, weighing all the options before committing herself. Charlie was always known to make rash choices, but she at least waited a few moments to ponder them. Sinclair knew how to manipulate her, for he had been doing it for years. He wouldn't have to wait long. She would come to him begging for his help.

Once he sat astride his horse, he nodded to Charlotte and rode off. He smiled when she could no longer see his expression. Yes, this would be an enjoyable house party after all.

Charlie fumed when Jasper rode away, not giving her a chance to reply. There had to be a way to accept his offer without selling Sapphire's foal. Charlie had planned to train the foal herself and had convinced Uncle Theo into allowing her.

Seeing Jasper approach the house and get off his horse, Charlie's temper rose to a degree in which she would need to remain there longer. When he turned to her and tipped his hat, Charlie uttered every name a proper lady would never speak. She didn't need Jasper Sinclair's assistance. She would get through this week without incident and once everyone left, she would resume a normal life. One without a groom.

Chapter Four

Charlotte sat next to Evelyn on the settee, watching Sinclair move from one eligible lady to the next. His charm would have each of them twittering like a silly chit. Even Jacqueline and Gemma, who had known him since childhood, fell for his charm. It was the other ladies Uncle Theo had invited whom he flirted with that unsettled Charlotte. Her uncle had only invited the other debutantes to fool the gentlemen about his agenda. However, every gentleman he'd invited had his seal of approval if they won their hands. Uncle Theo left nothing to chance.

A small gathering filled the library after dinner, since only a few of the guests had arrived. The rest would arrive tomorrow when the house party kicked into full swing. Aunt Susanna had the week filled with a variety of activities to keep the boredom away. Charlotte waited in anticipation for the ball. Then this complete farce would be over and she could return to her daily life.

Those days were filled with spending time with family and working with the horses. She would tackle the issue of going to London for the season when it grew closer. If she pretended to make every attempt at finding a husband and failed at the end, she could prove to Uncle Theo how hopeless a season would be. The only flaw in this plan was that she didn't want to encourage any of the gentlemen invited to the house party. So that left only Sinclair's offer.

If his actions were anything to go by, then he meant to make her grovel. Which she wouldn't do. Nor would she promise Sapphire's foal. She might lead him false that she would, but the foal *would* be hers once it was born. Uncle Theo had more than promised it would be. Tomorrow, during one of Aunt Susanna's activities, Charlie would inform Sinclair that she would accept the offer of help.

Or perhaps she could talk with him now, considering he made his way over to them?

Charlotte smoothed her skirts and flashed Sinclair an encouraging smile. However, the smile he returned was one of polite indifference. Now, a different smile he directed toward Evelyn held the same flirtatious charm he bestowed on all the other ladies.

"Ladies."

"Lord Sinclair," Evelyn said.

Charlie refused to answer the greeting. Evelyn elbowed her in the side for the discourtesy. Instead of replying, Charlie glared at Sinclair. Usually he would make a remark toward her unruly behavior, instead this time he continued to ignore Charlotte.

"Evelyn, would you be so kind to join me in a stroll through the gardens with Gray and Lady Selina? Your uncle and Lady Forrester will be in the walking party too."

"It would be my pleasure. Would you mind if Charlotte accompanied us?"

Before Sinclair answered, Charlotte spoke. "I am sorry, Evelyn, I must beg off. I promised Lord Worthington a game of chess."

"Excellent, I shall have you all to myself," Sinclair declared, helping Evelyn stand. He placed her hand in the crook of his arm and led them outside.

Evelyn looked over her shoulder with anger at Charlie for refusing to join them, knowing that Charlie lied. Charlie dropped her eyes, ashamed that she abandoned her twin to the scoundrel. But she wouldn't tag along only for Sinclair to ignore her.

Once the party began their stroll through the garden, Charlotte rose and walked outside. She watched how Sinclair bent his head to listen to Evelyn. Their steps had slowed, and they were an inappropriate distance from the rest of the group. Sinclair stopped and brushed a stray curl from Evelyn's cheek as he did earlier in the day to Charlotte. He bent and whispered something into Evelyn's ear. Instead of Evelyn slapping him, she laughed and they resumed their walk, catching up to the others. It would appear he had charmed her sister this evening too. Which left Charlie the only lady uncharmed by the scoundrel.

"Did I hear correctly that you promised me a game of chess?"

Charlotte pasted on a sweet smile and twirled around, embarrassed to be caught in her lie. "I am sorry, Lord Worthington, I fear I used you for an excuse. If it would please you, we can play a game."

Lord Worthington leaned closer and whispered, "Do you really want to play chess?"

Charlotte shook her head.

"Would you rather escape this boredom and visit the stables?"

Worthington knew Charlotte's weakness and tempted her with a stroll that would ruin her reputation if anyone caught them alone.

"If you take a few steps to the side, you would be out of the other guest's viewpoint. After a short time we can make our escape." Worthington further tempted Charlotte with a devious plan.

Charlotte scanned the room and noticed everyone's attention focused on a card game they were playing. She could easily slip away and nobody would notice. When Evelyn came back, she would assume that Charlotte had returned to their bedroom. A walk to the stables to visit Sapphire would be the highlight of the evening. Charlotte took a few steps deeper into the darkness. When after a while no one called out her name and the party from the garden couldn't see her, she nodded to Worthington, and he chuckled, drawing her hand to his elbow, leading them to the stables.

"I had hoped I could convince you to leave."

"You played on my one weakness, my lord."

"Only one weakness?"

"Of course."

"Mmm, I think you have at least one other weakness."

"Nonsense."

"Then Sinclair charming every lady this evening but you does not faze you? Or him singling out your sister for a stroll?"

"I do not understand your point. If this is how our visit to the stable will proceed, you may leave and I will find my own way." Charlotte pulled her hand from Worthington's elbow and stopped walking.

Worthington only laughed, drawing her hand back. "All right, I promise no more talk of Sinclair."

Once they reached the stables, Worthington led them to Sapphire's stall. The horse snickered in enjoyment at seeing Charlotte. She tried to nudge her for a treat.

"Sorry girl, this was a surprise visit."

"Perhaps she would enjoy this." Worthington held out an apple and a knife.

Charlotte beamed a smile at him. His thoughtfulness endeared him. While Charlotte fed Sapphire pieces of the apple Worthington peeled, she told him of her plans for the foal. He in turn told Charlotte of the horses in his stables. Their common interest erased thoughts of Sinclair from Charlie's mind.

Lord Reese Worthington was a schoolmate of Lucas's and had visited the estate occasionally. He always spent his time with Lucas, and Charlotte never had the opportunity to learn more about him. Perhaps this week wouldn't be so difficult to get through and she wouldn't need Sinclair's help. If she befriended Worthington, then he would be the gentleman she pretended to fall for. When the week was over, he would return home and she would have shown Uncle Theo how she'd attempted to socialize.

When the time came to return to the house, Worthington escorted Charlotte to where she could sneak inside undetected. He acted the perfect gentlemen, not once attempting anything inappropriate. They made plans to visit the stable tomorrow with a chaperone. He wanted her opinion on a matter concerning his horse. Worthington's company was a pleasant change from a certain other bachelor in attendance. Charlotte wished Worthington good evening and slipped inside, making her way to her bedroom. Charlotte opened the door and sighed in relief that Evelyn hadn't returned yet. No one would know of her visit to the stables with Worthington unchaperoned.

Charlie readied for bed without help from Polly and laid down waiting for Evelyn to return. She wanted to learn more of Evelyn's walk with Sinclair. Charlie had to make sure that her sister didn't fall for his wicked charm.

~~~~~~

Sinclair smoked his cigar, watching the couple walk to the rear of the house. The echoes of their animated conversation drifted in the air. When they reached the servant's entrance, the gentleman lifted the lady's hands and placed a kiss on her gloved fingers. Then he bent his head and whispered something in her ear. Worthington overstepped with the miss. This unsettled Sinclair. The bounder was poaching on his territory. The sight of Worthington charming Charlotte shouldn't bother him, except she was an innocent miss and Worthington was a rake. Otherwise, Charlotte meant nothing to Sinclair. Nothing at all.

So why did Sinclair feel the need to stake his claim on Charlotte? No, he had no intention of falling into the parson's noose. He only wanted the new foal from Sapphire. Obviously, that was Worthington's goal too. The lord's new stables and the breeding program he was starting was the talk in all the clubs. Sinclair needed to convince Charlie of his help so she didn't fall victim to a false courtship. Yes, he would protect her from Worthington and any other gentleman who attempted to woo her. But not before he issued a warning to Worthington first.

"I do not think the Duke of Colebourne would take kindly to one of his guests sneaking around with one of his wards in the dark of night."

"No, I do not suppose he would." Worthington continued to stride past Sinclair.

"Charlotte Holbrooke is not your usual conquest. What are your intentions with the chit?"

Worthington turned and smirked at Sinclair. "My intentions are none of your concern, Sinclair."

"Perhaps they are."

"Are you declaring your intentions for the lady?"

When Sinclair didn't answer, Worthington laughed.

"And you are mistaken. Charlotte Holbrooke is exactly my choice of a lady. She is fiery and feisty. The exact kind I find pleasure with between my bedsheets."

Sinclair scowled, dropping his cigar and smashing it under his Hessians. He intended to plant a facer on Worthington, but stopped himself. If Colebourne caught wind of an altercation, then Sinclair would be ordered home. Sinclair had finagled an invitation only through being a neighbor who spent the majority of his time at the Colebourne stables. The duke allowed him to learn the process of his breeding program so that Sinclair could start his own. With Sinclair joining their family for dinner on a weekly basis, it would have been impolite not to invite him.

Gray had made it clear to him that under no circumstances was he to ruin any chances for his cousins to find grooms. Gray had filled him in on the duke's plans since Sinclair caught Charlotte outside the window. He understood why the duke wanted the girls to settle. With his advancing age and health concerns over the last year, the duke worried over the ladies' security. Sinclair made a promise not to interfere. However, that didn't mean any promises on not pursuing any of the girls for himself. And if he had to pursue Charlie to protect her, then that would be his mission.

Anything to keep Charlotte out of Worthington's clutches.

Chapter Five

Charlie rolled over, looking over at Evelyn's bed. Her sister had already left to join everyone in Jacqueline's room for their morning ritual. The night before, Charlie had fallen asleep before Evelyn returned. She would have to wait until when they got dressed for the day to question Evelyn.

She walked next door to Jacqueline's bedroom and to the excited chatter of her family. Even Abigail, who had trepidations over the house party, seemed pleased with the guests Uncle Theo invited. Abigail discussed with Gemma about the other girls invited and how they were already forming friendships. Charlie smiled, pleased that Abigail now embraced the house party. Jacqueline and Evelyn had their heads bent close together, whispering. When Charlie wandered closer, they stopped talking.

"Good morning, Charlie," said Jacqueline.

"Good morning, sisters."

Evelyn slid over on the overstuffed chair, making room for Charlie. Charlie sat next to her, reaching for a scone. She had her mouth full of the berry delight exploding on her tongue when Jacqueline started questioning Charlotte on her absence.

"Where did you disappear to after Evelyn joined Sinclair for a walk?"

"I retired early due to a headache coming on."

"That is peculiar."

"What is?" Charlie asked between bites.

"I came to check on you, and your room was empty."

Charlie choked and Evelyn patted her on the back. Charlotte had assumed she was in the clear, since she'd returned before Evelyn. Charlie never thought about Jacqueline checking on her. She took a sip of hot chocolate before she lied some more.

With a calm to her voice that she didn't hold, Charlie replied, "You must have checked while I was requesting Mrs. Oakes to make me her special tincture."

Jacqueline continued staring at Charlie with a motherly *I know you are fibbing* look. Then there was Evelyn's *why are you deceiving Jacqueline* stare. Charlie's only response was to feign innocence. She would need to find Mrs. Oakes and bribe the housekeeper with her favorite sweet—which would require a special trip to the village to buy the peppermints Mrs. Oakes so enjoyed.

"You did not sneak off to the stables with Lord Worthington, did you?" Jacqueline whispered low enough so that Gemma and Abigail couldn't hear.

"No. That would be inappropriate behavior that I promised you I would not partake in. I had a simple headache, that was all."

"Promise?"

Charlie hated lying to her sisters. "I promise."

Before Jacqueline reminded them again of the need for proper behavior, the peaceful atmosphere in the room evaporated.

Selina was at the door.

"How quaint that you ladies still partake in this childish ritual. I would have figured you'd outgrown the need for security. And it is so generous that you include Miss Cason, considering she should be at work below stairs. That is, unless she is the one serving you ladies, then her company explains all."

The shrew had arrived at the house party and came bearing her claws. Her cutting remark toward Abigail was inexcusable. Charlie swore to herself that before the house party ended, she would seek revenge against Lucas's betrothed.

Abigail impressed Charlie with a calm demeanor. But she saw the hurt and doubt cloud Abigail's eyes. Selina Pemberton never missed an opportunity to remind Abigail of her place in society. But what Selina always seemed to forget was how Abigail's family always protected her. Oh, they wouldn't waste their time with words. No, they'd learned their lesson with Selina on the battling of wits. The miss had too much practice on being vindictive, and they were no match. Instead they would seek revenge on Selina in more practical ways. Ways that would reflect poorly on her, and always in front of others.

"Would you care to join us?" Abigail asked.

None of them had ever invited Selina to join their circle. When Aunt Susanna prepared them for the house party, she offered one piece of advice, saying that ladies from London were of a different variety than the friends they had made in the village who were of a sort to accept life as they knew it. The ladies in the ton were raised with one purpose and one purpose only. And that was to secure themselves with a match higher than the one they were born into. But for them not to think *all* the ladies were of a competitive nature, some would make excellent friends. So they weren't to guard their feelings too closely. However, still to be aware of nefarious characters.

Aunt Susanna said to kill them with kindness, even when they were anything but. It would seem Abigail was applying Aunt Susanna's advice toward Selina.

Abigail's question seemed to take Selina aback. They waited in bated breath. The beauty narrowed her eyes, looking each girl square in the face. They each bestowed a smile of acceptance.

"Why would I want to join this gathering when Lucas invited me to join him for breakfast on his private terrace?" Selina directed the snub directly at Abigail.

Abigail said, "Then I hope your breakfast with Lucas is enjoyable. Please accept our invitation to join us tomorrow morning for hot chocolate and scones. We will be in the twin's bedroom. It was remiss of us not to invite you or the other ladies while the house party was in session. Please accept our apologies for excluding you over the years."

Selina's only reply was a humph before she walked away. She had intended to ruin their morning ritual, instead it had backfired. Poor Lucas. Selina would make the breakfast miserable. Charlie held no sympathy for her cousin. Those two deserved each other. Charlie still hadn't forgiven Lucas over his comments regarding Abigail enjoying a season. She would have loved to sneak out and watch them, but she'd made a promise of no eavesdropping during the house party. Charlie had made a lot of promises recently. They were becoming hard to keep. However, she would continue trying.

"Kill them with kindness," Abigail said, before anyone asked.

They all fell into a fit of giggles at Abigail's impression of Aunt Susanna. It did no good to discuss Selina's spitefulness. An act they were used to, and would have to endure more after her marriage to Lucas. They'd also learned not to waste their energy trying to understand Selina.

Soon they dispersed to their rooms to dress for the day. The rest of the guests were set to arrive later that morning and Aunt Susanna planned an afternoon of entertainment. Charlie followed Evelyn into the bedroom where Polly waited to help them dress. Her sister didn't say anything until Polly left to help Jacqueline get ready.

"Why did you lie to Jacqueline, and where did you sneak away to last night?"

"Because I did accept Lord Worthington's offer to visit the stables. It was innocent, but Jacqueline would have deemed it inappropriate."

"That is because it was."

"Nonsense. We visited Sapphire, talked about horses, and Worthington walked me to the servant's quarters, where I snuck in unnoticed."

"Nothing untoward happened?"

"Nothing. Well, except ..."

"Except what?"

"He kissed my hand before I slipped inside."

"Charlie!"

"Evelyn, it was an innocent gesture, nothing more. Now, how was your walk with Sinclair? What did you discuss? Did he mention me?"

"It was pleasant. We discussed the events planned for the week. Why would your name come up in our discussion?"

Charlie pretended to straighten the hair ribbons on the vanity they shared. "No reason."

"Charlie?"

Evelyn waited for Charlie to reply. Charlie couldn't keep anything from her twin. Not that she wanted to. Or did she? What would Evelyn think of Sinclair's offer? Would she approve?

"Yesterday, Sinclair offered to pretend interest in a courtship between us so I would not have to endure the torture of other gentlemen's attention. In exchange for my persuasion to Uncle Theo to sell Sapphire's foal to Sinclair."

"Did you agree?"

"No. Then I changed my mind after he rode off. However, I couldn't get his attention the entire evening to agree. Then, when he asked you to join him on the stroll through the gardens, I knew I lost my chance. However, when Worthington coaxed me into visiting the stables, I decided I might not need Sinclair. Worthington is a nice enough chap and we hold a common interest. I do not think he wants a wife. I can spend time with him instead, and once the house party has ended, I will have convinced Uncle Theo that I attempted to take part, but the gentlemen did not take to me. So a season would be a mistake, and he will leave me behind."

"What interests do you hold with Lord Worthington?"

"Horses."

"Oh," Evelyn answered softly.

"Yes, he has started this breeding program that is revolutionary. When I asked him questions, he was patient with me until I understood what he discussed. Never once growling at me, unlike Sinclair. He even wants my advice on his horse later today. I promise I will take a chaperone this time. You never answered *my* question. Did Sinclair mention my name or not?"

"No, Charlotte, he did not."

Charlie should have felt relief that Sinclair had forgotten about their offer. However, she only experienced a sense of loss. Was he interested in Evelyn? Was Evelyn interested in Sinclair?

"Are you interested in him, Evelyn?"

"Who, Lord Worthington? We have nothing in common. I tolerate horses when I must. He loves them. I am shy and quiet, afraid to talk to gentlemen. He is outgoing and charms every female within his sight. I blend into the shadows, while he is a perfect specimen of the male form. With those broad shoulders, muscled thighs, a smile that makes your heart flutter, and his thick, blond waves with its tousled look. A head of hair where you would like to run your fingers through while he plunders your mouth with a kiss ..." Evelyn ended on one of her sighs.

Charlie stared at Evelyn in shock. Her sister's reading material of late must be very scandalous, because Evelyn's description of Lord Worthington answered Charlie's question. No, Evelyn wasn't interested in Sinclair, but Worthington. How had Charlie not seen this? She thought they shared everything. It would appear Evelyn kept a few secrets of her own. Charlie had watched the dreamy expression in her sister's eyes while she described Worthington and knew Evelyn was in love with the earl. Now, Charlie wouldn't be able to use Worthington to her advantage. Or could she?

Charlie said, "Actually, I was referring to Sinclair."

Evelyn blushed and strode to the window to cool herself. "We should go below stairs or Aunt Susanna will send a search party for us."

"Evelyn."

Evelyn sighed and turned around. "Charlotte."

"You love him."

"Sinclair? Nonsense, the gentleman is like a brother to us."

"I was referring to Lord Worthington *this* time."

Evelyn closed her eyes before admitting. "Yes."

Charlie rushed over and enveloped Evelyn in a hug. Evelyn relaxed in her arms.

"'Tis silly," said Evelyn.

"'Tis wonderful. How long have you been in love with Worthington?"

"Do you remember when he visited over the Christmas holidays?"

"Yes."

Evelyn withdrew from Charlie.

"Well, we might have shared a kiss under the mistletoe."

"Might have? And you never thought to share this with me?"

"It was too personal, Charlie."

"I understand. Now that you have mentioned the kiss, you must spill the rest."

Charlie settled in a chair, pulling her legs up to rest her chin on her knees, waiting in anticipation. Evelyn must have realized Charlie wouldn't leave until she told everything, because Evelyn sat too.

"I was unable to sleep, and I did not want to disturb you. So, I went to the library to get a book to read. When I entered the library, it was to find Lord Worthington drinking near the fire. I tried to turn and leave before he noticed me, but I was not quick enough."

"Did he sweep you off your feet?"

"Not at first. I apologized for interrupting him and tried to return upstairs. He stopped me under the door and teased me about the mistletoe. He said, as an apology on invading his solitude, I must kiss him for forgiveness. I knew he was only jesting, but his manner was so inviting. He lured me closer and whispered how much he had wanted to kiss me since dinner. Which only confused me, because I didn't sit near him at dinner. I lost all sense of right and wrong when his arms wrapped around me and his mouth lowered to mine. When his lips met mine, it was like finally coming home."

"How romantic," Charlie sighed.

"Mmm."

"How did it feel to be kissed?"

"Wonderful. Exhilarating. Wanted. Loved. But most of all disappointing."

"Disappointing? Why?"

"Because it was not my name he whispered after the kiss."

"Why, that scoundrel. If not yours, then whose?"

"Yours," Evelyn whispered.

"Mine? That is absurd."

"You do not remember, do you?"

"Remember what?

"You were the one who sat next to him at dinner that night. It was your animated discussion of Sapphire that entranced him. He sat next to you when we sang Christmas carols. Worthington thought he was kissing *you* under the mistletoe. With him seeking your attention last night, it only shows proof on who he desires. 'Tis not I."

"Oh, Evelyn. I am sorry. I held no clue."

"How would you? You are not at fault."

"What happened after he whispered my name? Did you slap him?"

Evelyn shook her head.

"Did you call him out?"

Evelyn looked away from Charlie.

"Evelyn, what did you do?"

"I might have allowed him a few more liberties than I should have. It is not what you're thinking, Charlotte. Only a few more kisses, perhaps, while I sat on his lap."

 "This is madness."

Charlie exploded out of her chair and paced across the bedroom. She stopped from time to time, shaking her head at Evelyn, before resuming her stride. This was a complete utter madness. Not only had her sister compromised herself, but the scoundrel believed it was Charlie he seduced. No wonder he'd sought her attention last night. Worthington assumed he could pick up where he left off. He would be in for a disappointment. Charlie should be cross with Evelyn, but when Evelyn described her time with Worthington, she'd noticed a difference. That one kiss brought Evelyn out of her shell. A shell she had burrowed in since their parent's death. While Charlie rebelled at every opportunity, Evelyn locked herself away. If this was the gentleman who could show Evelyn how to live, then Charlie would sacrifice her good name for love to happen. Charlie stopped in front of Evelyn.

"Why did you not at least tell him who he was kissing?"

"Because I was afraid he would stop once he realized he held the unnoticeable twin on his lap. He wanted the wild twin. I was afraid to see disappointment in his eyes, not the flare of desire burning directly at me. I cannot even describe the sensation of his arms holding me in their embrace. The emotions overwhelmed any rational thought. I only wanted to *feel*. I am sorry for the deception. Please forgive me."

Charlie grabbed Evelyn's hands in hers.

"There is nothing to forgive. In fact, I am most impressed. I finally have rubbed off on you. And in such a naughty way too." Charlie laughed.

"Have you ever …?"

"No, never. That is what makes this so grand."

"Please, do not tell a soul. I made a promise to myself not to pine over Worthington and to overcome my shyness by engaging with the other gentlemen that Uncle Theo has invited."

"I promise your secret is safe with me. What if you can have your fun with Worthington *and* show him your charm, not mine, and also make him jealous enough to pursue you?"

"That sounds deceitful, and that is not how I wish to make him fall in love with me."

"Hear me out, sister. I am only suggesting on occasions we trade places like we used to when we were younger. No one could tell the difference then, and I doubt if they could now. The only challenging aspect would be that when you are pretending to be me, you must embrace the full Charlotte Holbrooke experience."

"This does not sound wise. I fear the consequences, if anyone catches our deceit."

"Then we must make sure we never get caught. Shall we win you the love of Lord Worthington?"

Evelyn nodded, too choked up to speak. The love for Worthington shone from her eyes while Charlie explained their plan. When they joined the family to greet the guests for the day, they would do so as themselves. Aunt Susanna planned a game of pall mall for the afternoon where she would split them into teams of a gentleman and lady each. Charlie told Evelyn that she would convince Aunt Susanna to pair Evelyn with Sinclair, and herself with Worthington. Then, before they went outside, they would make the switch with their clothing. Evelyn would then play the game with Worthington and win him over. While Charlie would pretend to be Evelyn with Sinclair.

She couldn't wait to fool the marquess. Sinclair didn't realize it yet, but he would end up helping her *and* Evelyn at the same time—with no knowledge of his assistance.

Chapter Six

Sinclair waited for Evelyn to join him out on the lawn. He held their mallets. When Charlotte had rejoined the group, he thought Evelyn wouldn't be far behind. The two sisters had excused themselves with a need to gather their bonnets, but an excuse was all it was. Charlie had emerged with her hair flowing behind her. Her display of enthusiasm for having Worthington for a partner was nauseating. If anything, she tried too hard. But it fooled Worthington, if his smirk in Sinclair's direction was anything to go by. Sinclair tried to persuade Lady Forrester into letting Charlie and him partner. However, the lady had been adamant about the teams being picked and they were final. Perhaps he would use this to his advantage. He would ply information from Evelyn about Charlotte and Worthington. Then he would plan on how to come between them.

"Please forgive my delay, Lord Sinclair," Evelyn spoke quietly behind him.

Evelyn had at least grabbed a bonnet to protect her skin, unlike her sister. The pale blue matched her cream-colored dress to perfection. Even though they were twins, their mannerisms were different. Jasper had always been able to tell them apart. However, something seemed off with Evelyn this afternoon. He tried to catch her gaze, but Evelyn kept her head lowered, looking down where he had been rolling the ball under his boot. Sinclair wanted to reassure Evelyn that his impatience wasn't because of her. When she still wouldn't make eye contact with him, he placed a knuckle under her chin and raised her head.

When his eyes connected with Evelyn's they sparked with the same damn attraction he felt for her sister. Sinclair jerked his finger away and stepped back. Shame settled over him for experiencing the same lust for sisters. Sinclair would need to pay a visit to the widow Chambers soon. Obviously, his absence from bedding a woman these last couple of months affected his libido. Not only did he want to kiss one Holbrooke lady, now he wanted to kiss two of them.

Sinclair almost made a fool of himself with Evelyn until she tilted her head to the side. There was only one twin who held this characteristic. And that was Charlie. With a quick perusal, he took notice of a few changes that he wouldn't have seen otherwise, except he hadn't taken his eyes off of Charlotte Holbrooke all day. He tried to engage with her, but she kept avoiding him.

The most noticeable of changes was the shawl. They had changed their dresses, but they neglected to swap out the shawls. Then there was the matter of their hairstyles. While both girls had worn their hair down from earlier, they forgot to change the ribbons. Charlie still had the same green ribbon peeking out of her bonnet. Where before Evelyn had been wearing yellow ribbons in her hair. He looked over Charlie's shoulder and sure enough, without a bonnet to contain them, those yellow ribbons were floating in the air behind Evelyn. Then the most prominent feature was the color of their eyes. He couldn't for the life of him remember the color of Evelyn's. When the spark of attention caused him to drop his fingers, he had stared into the greenest eyes with flecks of gold. Charlotte's eyes.

"A worthwhile wait, for your beauty has humbled the very air I breathe, sweet Evelyn."

A blush spread across Charlie's cheeks and she lowered her lashes. Sinclair wanted to laugh at the demure expression, but decided to have some fun for a bit. He wouldn't hold out for long, but long enough to make Charlie wonder if he held an interest in Evelyn.

"Shall we?" Sinclair bent to pick up the ball and crooked his elbow.

Charlie slid a hand along his arm. She remained quiet after his compliment, the way Evelyn would. However, Sinclair was no longer fooled. The heat from her touch radiated off his arm. A heat only enflamed around Charlotte. A heat he wanted to explore. Why, after all this time, he held no clue. Another gentleman's interest toward Charlotte didn't sit well with him. Also, he had noticed the remaining bachelor's glances toward her when introductions were made. He saw their sparks of interests. Sparks he would extinguish when needed.

On the path to join the others, he plied Charlie with a steady stream of conversation. Each comment more flirtatious than the one before. While not obnoxious, he hoped to draw out Charlie's temper. However, the chit stood strong in her deceit. If he hadn't known Charlie like he did, the twins would have fooled him too. She played Evelyn to perfection. Each answer was polite and quiet, with her blushes growing darker.

When they reached the course, the game had already begun, and they were the last players to start. Each team traded off on the players to hit the ball toward the round wire. Sinclair placed the ball in Charlie's hand, his fingers laying on top of hers longer than he should have, hoping to fluster her. If she had been Evelyn it would have worked, which only proved he was correct on Charlie's identity. Charlie's confidence on her deception must have been bolstered during the short walk. Because of instead of pulling away in shyness, she smiled at him. Not the victorious smile of Charlie, but one of Evelyn's smiles. Sweet, patient, and full of innocence.

She lowered the ball to the ground, placing it where she wanted to hit it. When she bent over, the shawl dropped from her shoulders. The tips of the cashmere lace dangled near the grass. That was when Sinclair noted the last clue. The buttons were in the wrong holes on the back of the dress and two of the holes were missing buttons altogether. In their haste to switch clothing, Charlie and Evelyn forgot a few minor details. Sinclair bit back his laughter. Charlie rose, and he handed her the mallet.

Charlie started off the game with the first whack. They took turns trying to catch up with the rest of the party, but the other players pulled ahead. When Sinclair looked around, he noticed the guests were laughing and enjoying their partners in the game. None of the guests paid them any attention. They were near the outskirts of the open lawn. Next to them were trees and bushes, leading to a pond nearby.

Sinclair stood back while Charlie tilted her head to the side, trying to decide the best strategy. If she hit it to the left too hard, it risked flying into the wooded area. However, if she hit it toward the right too much, they would be off course, putting them farther behind. She paused, wiggling her hips into position, causing Sinclair to groan. The innocent act flared his imagination with carnal thoughts. When she hesitated on hitting the ball, Sinclair came behind Charlie and pressed himself against her backside. He slid his hands down her arms, wrapping them around hers. Her body stiffened.

"You must tap the ball lightly. Or else we will have to search for it in the trees," Sinclair whispered near Charlie's ear.

Charlie's heart stopped for a brief second, before it rapidly pounded again in her chest. Once it regained, she held her breath. Sinclair had wrapped his body around hers while instructing how to hit the ball. Charlie *knew* how to hit the ball. She didn't know how to deal with Sinclair so close.

His warm breath against her neck melted her insides. His fingers were now sliding in between hers, holding the mallet with her. She felt his manhood against her backside. Charlie had been around horses enough to understand that Sinclair held desire for her. Charlie paused. Not for her. For Evelyn. This unsettled Charlie even more. The marquess's invitation for a stroll the night before, and his attention throughout the game, made his interest in Evelyn clear.

Charlie must put a stop to his behavior. She couldn't think with him so close. After the game, she would find a quiet spot and reflect on how Sinclair's desire for Evelyn affected her. Then she would find Evelyn and inform her of Sinclair's interest. It was the only fair thing to do. Once she told Evelyn, she would confess to Sinclair of their deception. Then if he truly wanted Evelyn, he would have to win her heart, even though Charlie knew Evelyn's heart held out for Worthington. While Charlie thought she could deceive others, her conscience always won.

She pulled herself out of his embrace. Charlie glanced around and saw no one paid them any attention. When her gaze landed on Sinclair, it was to find his devilish, charming, flirtatious, sinful smile directed on her.

"Lord Sinclair, your assistance is not needed," Charlotte stuttered. She didn't have to pretend to be Evelyn. Sinclair's smile flustered her beyond all reason. Which only made him smile more.

Sinclair held his hands up. "My apologies again, sweet Evelyn. Once again your beauty overtook all rational thought."

Charlie felt the blush spread across her cheeks at his flattery. When he stepped back to allow her to hit, she made sure not to dawdle. If Sinclair were to touch her again or whisper in her ear, she would become a muddled mess on her uncle's lawn. With everyone to witness.

Just as she swung the mallet back, ready to hit the ball, Sinclair ran his fingers along the buttons on the back of her dress. "A piece of advice, my dear."

Charlie closed her eyes and gulped when Sinclair slid the buttons undone on her dress. The mallet hung in the air. Sinclair's actions scandalized her, where anyone could see. However, Charlie secretly wished he would slide his fingers inside the dress and caress her with his gentle touch.

"Yes?" she whispered.

Then as quickly as he unbuttoned the dress, he slid them closed again. "The next time you switch places with Evelyn, make sure your dress is in proper order, Charlotte."

Charlie's eyes flew open and she swung the mallet, smacking the ball so hard it flew into the trees. The devil. Sinclair had played her. Charlie thought she had fooled Sinclair, only for him to play his own game at her expense. She turned and glared at him.

"I warned you to tap it lightly."

Charlie scowled and stomped off toward the trees. She swung the mallet back and forth across the weeds, slicing it through the air. Her anger directed at the wilderness, when it should be at the irritating lord she'd walked away from. The very one she heard following, his laughter echoing. She wasn't even looking for the ball, only trying to vent her frustration.

Sinclair followed Charlie in her rant as she destroyed the poor wildflowers in her path. He almost ran into her when she spun and started advancing on him. She held onto the base of the mallet and pointed the end at him. Charlie poked him in the chest, snarling. She was a tempting package when she was feisty. Sinclair enjoyed frustrating Charlie.

"You knew all along." With each word she tapped him on the chest.

Sinclair yanked at the stick, pulling Charlie closer. Once he reached the base, he peeled her hands away and dropped the mallet at their feet. He drew her into his embrace, lowering his mouth but a breath away from hers. Sinclair caught the hitch in Charlotte's breath through his lips. He watched her mouth tremble. His only answer was to draw her lips between his. When she opened her mouth in astonishment, he slid his tongue inside to stroke slowly. Savoring every delicious flavor of Charlotte Holbrooke. Her response surprised him when she slid her hands through his hair and drew him closer. When she moaned, Sinclair was lost. He devoured Charlie, drawing one kiss after another. Each moan lasted longer than the one from before. Each one of his kisses stroked the flames higher to hear the whisper of her pleasure. Charlotte consumed his senses, making him lose all practical sense to their location. Sinclair needed to withdraw and put distance between them, but his senses fought against him. Only one more kiss he promised, then he would stop. Sinclair needed to stop before he did something so foolish that it would have him married to Charlotte. What he truly desired was to lay her amongst the wildflowers and show how he knew it was her and not Evelyn all long.

Sinclair had finally accomplished what Charlie had fought against over the last few months whenever she was near him. He had turned her into a muddled state of confusion. No, he made her curious. No, he ignited her desire. His kisses melted her insides and flamed her senses. They became more demanding with each stroke of his tongue, as if he couldn't get enough of her. Charlie only knew she wanted more. When she sensed that he would pull away, she clung tighter. When his lips withdrew, her tongue slid slowly across his lips, tasting him. Jasper tasted of the warm afternoon sun mixed with sin. A taste Charlie never wanted to end. Her tongue slid inside and then back again to his lips. When she repeated, he growled and pulled her closer, devouring her.

Charlie's innocent exploration pushed his restraint past the need to be a gentleman. He wanted her with a need so powerful he wouldn't be able to control. This was madness. He pushed her away from him before he acted on his desires. Sinclair strode away, putting much needed distance between them. He ran his fingers through his hair over and over, his steps taking him up the hill. Sinclair fought with his control, trying to rationalize what in the hell had just happened.

Why did Charlotte, of all women, make him want to lose control? He had a plan for this week. That was to persuade her to help him gain ownership of a horse. Instead, one kiss that Sinclair meant to only tease Charlie with, had exploded into a sensation of ecstasy. Her innocent response, her needful moans, the stroking of her fingers through his hair, undid him. Sinclair turned to the source of his frustration.

Charlie stood in the meadows with her fingers held to her lips. The bonnet she had worn to hide her identity lay at her feet. During their kiss, he must have taken it off. Even from this distance, she held the look of a woman who had been ravished. Her wide eyes, swollen lips, and tousled hair lay proof of the kiss they shared. Nay, kisses. Sinclair couldn't stop at one. He was a greedy bastard that took more. What made him even more selfish was the need to make Charlotte his.

~~~~~~

Charlotte watched Jasper trudge up the hill. She couldn't move to save herself. With each step he took away from her, Charlotte lost a piece of herself. When his lips took possession of hers, she gave him a piece of her soul. She had experienced nothing so powerful before. Her body stood crying for him. Even though he was near, the need to have him closer overtook her senses.

Why of all the gentlemen in attendance did Jasper Sinclair have to be the one who awakened her? After losing her parents, Charlotte had only gone through the motions to get through life. While she projected the image of being carefree and adventurous, she was anything but. She was scared to love. Scared to be loved. Why did Jasper have to kiss her?

Charlie ran her fingers over where his lips had caressed hers. She felt the warmth of Jasper. The rest of her body tingled from being held so close to him. Her body stood yearning with an unfamiliar ache, begging for him to return. Only he wouldn't.

"Evelyn," Charlie heard her sister calling. "Evelyn, where are you? You are missing tea. Lord Sinclair?"

Charlotte locked eyes with Jasper. She didn't understand his expression. Charlie titled her head to the side. It wasn't one of guilt, but it also wasn't one of pleasure. He looked disappointed. In himself? Or her?

"*Charlie,*" Evelyn hissed, trying to draw Charlie's attention away from Sinclair.

"Mmm."

"Charlie," Evelyn whispered with more emphasis. "What happened?"

"He kissed me."

"Sinclair?"

"Yes," Charlie sighed.

"Oh my. Charlotte, you must return with me, your whereabouts are being whispered amongst the guests."

Charlie wouldn't look away from Jasper. His regard haunted her. Even when Evelyn picked up the bonnet and fixed her hair, putting Charlie's dress to rights. Jasper disappeared over the ridge, and Charlie kept staring. Evelyn tugged at Charlie to follow her, muttering about marquesses, scandals, and Charlotte's ruination.

"We must return now."

"Evelyn."

Evelyn stopped. "Yes, dear?"

"I now understand what you described this morning about the effect of Worthington's kiss. You know when you said it was like coming home?"

"Yes."

"Yes," Charlie sighed.

"Oh, Charlotte."

"He knew the entire time."

"Knew what?" Evelyn asked, picking up the discarded mallet and searching for the ball. Once she located them they continued back into the open lawn. Charlie kept glancing over her shoulder for any sign of Sinclair. When he never reappeared, Charlie lost hope. Did she scare him away with her forwardness?

"That we had switched places."

"How? No one else guessed."

"Sinclair did not reveal how he figured out the difference."

"Did you ask?"

"I accused him of it, then in the next moment he pulled me into his arms and kissed me."

"Did you slap him?"

"No. I kissed him back."

"You did what?"

By this time they had arrived near the steps to the terrace. Charlotte couldn't answer any more of Evelyn's questions without revealing their switched identities. Charlotte would have to answer to Evelyn later, but for now Aunt Susanna's questions of her disappearance saved her. Luckily, Evelyn was quick on her toes and answered for her, displaying the lost ball and mallet. She explained how Sinclair had abandoned her sister to search for the ball herself. It was deep in the weeds, and she had lost time trying to search for it. Evelyn explained how her sister was embarrassed by Sinclair's abandonment and hence the reason for her delay. It was the most Evelyn has ever talked in front of a group of people before. Many who she wasn't acquainted with. However, Evelyn wasn't herself—she was Charlotte for the afternoon.

Throughout the rest of the day, Charlie sat in a daze, replaying the touch of Sinclair's lips on her own. His taste, his scent, his arms clutching her tight. She kept placing her fingers on her lips. Sinclair never rejoined them. She wondered if he would be at dinner. Evelyn kept her worried gaze upon her and tried to draw her into the conversations. However, Charlie stayed silent. It would appear the sisters did more than trade dresses for the afternoon. They changed personalities too.

Chapter Seven

For the past two days, Sinclair had made himself scarce. He joined the other guests for meals and the occasional discussions with the gentlemen over hunting, politics, and horses. However, he avoided the matchmaking activities and Charlotte at every opportunity. Not that the miss tried to seek his attention. No, she avoided him too. Though, her eyes betrayed that. Jasper would find her staring at him from afar. And he was aware of this because his gaze never wandered far from her. Charlie's gaze would skirt away whenever their eyes collided. Then there were his foolish thoughts. Jasper kept remembering their kiss. The simple kiss that awoke the need to make her his. An act that confused him, yet made him yearn to discover the depth of their desire.

Jasper thought if he stayed he could pretend indifference, but whenever another gentleman paid any attention toward Charlie, all he saw was green. Even if she only returned their kindness with a polite indifference, he still wanted her attention directed his way. Which she never would, because he avoided her at all costs. However, if any gentlemen continued a conversation with her for an obscene amount of time, he would interrupt them. Then he would draw the gentleman away from Charlie into another discussion.

Even now he wanted to interject himself in the conversation she held with Worthington. They were discussing horses, a topic Charlie would spend hours talking about. Worthington treated her as an equal in the discussion, which was the reason for their constant interaction during this affair. When Gray joined his cousin, something he said drew a blush across Charlie's cheeks and a smile of victory across Worthington's. The bounder made a comment and Charlie's blush grew rosier.

When the three of them disappeared out the door, Sinclair followed. Staying at a discreet distance, he kept close. When they disappeared into the stables, Sinclair stopped. He didn't need to continue to know they were going to visit Sapphire. What other reason would they have to visit the stables? He hung back in the shadows to wait for them. Sinclair reasoned to himself that he only waited to make sure Worthington didn't step out of line. He leaned against the stable, waiting, when he noticed someone sneaking in the shadows. He stepped around the side of the barn to see the figure struggling to stay hidden, constantly tugging her dress higher while walking at a hurried pace. When she drew closer, Sinclair's curiosity was appeased. Evelyn paused outside the doors, catching her breath and straightening her gown.

Sinclair's gaze narrowed when he took in the dress and the style of her hair. During dinner, Evelyn had worn a blue muslin with ribbons woven through her hair. Now she wore the same shade of dress as her sister, and her hair lay loose around her shoulders. What game did she play? No, what game did the sisters play? Evelyn glanced around to make sure no one saw her sneaking inside. Sinclair waited for a few seconds before he followed Evelyn, sticking to the darkness. Evelyn slipped inside an empty stall, and before long he heard the familiar whistle the twins would use to communicate with each other. Sinclair only held knowledge of this quirk after spending time with Charlotte learning about the duke's breeding program. Whenever Evelyn needed Charlie's attention she would mimic the whistle of a robin. Then Charlie would make her excuses to leave. Only this time the whistle was used for a distraction.

Sinclair watched the two women switch places so effortlessly that he wondered if he had ever been duped by them before. Charlie slid inside the stall with an excuse to grab a brush, and Evelyn exited with the brush held in her hand. When Evelyn approached Worthington and Gray, she accidently dropped the brush, keeping her distance from Sapphire. Sure, Worthington was a dimwit they could play false, but did they believe they would fool Gray? While Charlie was a natural around horses, they made Evelyn nervous.

Evelyn and Worthington bent over at the same time to retrieve the brush, and their heads bounced off each other. Evelyn giggled softly. Worthington's hands reached out and steadied Evelyn, smiling charmingly at her. Did he not realize the difference in the ladies' laughter? The softness of Evelyn's compared to the throaty one of Charlie's. Yes, the man was a dim-witted fool who didn't see the differences between the two. And that was what the twins played upon. But why?

Gray suggested that the party return to the house and turned to leave. Sinclair pressed deeper into the darkness. Evelyn smiled dreamily at Worthington, and he slid her arm into the crook of his, leading them back to the house. Their steps grew slower behind Gray's. For a moment it appeared as if Worthington meant to kiss Evelyn. Then Gray called over his shoulder for them to hurry along, breaking the moment.

A sigh behind him drew his attention to Charlie. She leaned smiling against the stall opening, watching her sister. Charlie retrieved the brush off the stool and stroked the bristles against Sapphire's coat. With each gentle movement, she whispered her thoughts out loud to the horse.

"While I find the man an absolute boar, Evelyn loves him."

Sapphire humphed, if horses could humph.

"'Tis true, Sapphire. And I know we play him false, with switching identities, but you should see the change in Evelyn. Worthington draws Evelyn out of her shell."

Sapphire snickered in agreement. That was, if horses could agree.

"It is only for a few more days, then she will tell him the truth after the ball. So bear with her until then. I promise you, I will make it worth your while."

Sinclair had moved closer. "And how will you make it worth my while to keep your secret?"

Charlie paused with the brush hanging in the air mid-stroke. She closed her eyes, savoring his nearness. The heat of Sinclair invaded her senses. After two days of Sinclair avoiding her, she wanted to throw herself in his arms. She missed him. However, his comment kept her facing away. They had fooled everyone else. Why not him? His comment should scare her, however the seductive question washed over Charlotte, tempting her to wonder if Sinclair felt the same attraction toward her.

Charlie slowly turned around to face Sinclair. Her breath hitched at the desire gleaming in his eyes. They spoke of a passion she wanted to explore. But they also held a determination that set her off balance. When she took a step back, Sinclair took a step forward until Charlie hit the wall.

"Well, Charlie?"

Charlie gulped. "Well what?"

"How will you keep my silence on Evelyn and your deception?"

Sinclair brushed the hair off her cheeks. The singe traveled to the tips of her toes. Could she be so bold to suggest what she desired? Would he think her too forward? When his fingers trailed down her neck, Charlie's confidence grew.

"Why, Lord Sinclair, you're suggesting something most scandalous?"

"I have suggested nothing, my dear. However, it would appear *your* thoughts are running toward a scandalous nature."

A blush stole across Charlie's cheeks.

"No, I um …" Charlie stammered.

"What did he say to you to make you blush?" Sinclair demanded.

Sinclair's change in the conversation confused Charlie. One second she was becoming that muddled pool of confusion around him with his sensuous words, the next he acted the jealous suitor.

"Who?"

"Worthington," Sinclair growled.

"When?"

"In the parlor, before you came outside."

"I did not blush."

"I saw you."

"You were watching me?" Charlie tilted her head to the side.

"What did he say?"

Charlie blew out a breath and mumbled, "He said the sparkle in my eyes was like a thousand twinkling stars shining down on him."

Jasper scoffed, "That rubbish made you blush?"

"It was not rubbish, it was poetic."

"Did that work on you?"

"Perhaps it did."

"No, I do not think so. You blushed, not because it flattered you, but his attention embarrassed you."

"Nonsense. I find Lord Worthington's attention charming."

"No, those soft words would make Evelyn swoon. But no, my dear, that compliment did nothing for you. You need to hear the fire of passion as it consumes your soul. You do not need words to make you blush, but you need the simple touch of a man who lights that fire. The kiss from a man who builds the flame higher until it consumes the very air you breathe. No words will do. Only the whirlwind of an emotion that can never be explained. Then and only then will you blush. Not from pure maidenhood, but from the pleasure of being a woman."

Jasper's words washed over Charlotte, making her weak in the knees. His head had lowered when he softly spoke to her, and a hand stroked her arm. The gentle caress emphasized each emotion he spoke of. Charlie stepped closer, lifting her head for a kiss. He brushed his thumb across her lips.

"I will not kiss you, Charlie."

"You're not?"

"No."

"I thought …"

"I know what you thought. However, what I want is for you to convince your uncle to sell me the foal for my silence on your little ruse."

"That is blackmail."

"No, a fair exchange."

Charlie growled, stepping away from his spell. The man was despicable. He twisted her innocent infatuation to his agenda. When he spoke of desire, passion, and the fire consuming them, she thought he cared for her. Especially after the kiss they shared. Instead, he only wanted to use her.

"What makes you think Uncle Theo would believe you over his own nieces?"

"Simple, I will tell him what I have observed. Then I will tell Worthington of your switching identities. He will not take the act lightly.

Worthington is a proud man. I will take pleasure in rubbing his nose in the fact that not one, but two lovely ladies duped him."

"You cannot tell Worthington."

"Give me one good reason not to."

Under any other circumstances, Charlotte wouldn't betray her sister, but she couldn't let Sinclair ruin what progress she had made with Worthington for Evelyn either. Her sister would just have to understand. Jasper had a soft spot for Evelyn ever since he'd rescued her from a spooked horse. He protected Evelyn like a brother, always making sure she was at ease around the horses, never leaving her alone with them.

"Evelyn loves him."

"Who, Worthington?"

"Yes."

"Why in the hell does she care for him? Does she know what kind of rake he is? His reputation in London is one of a scoundrel."

"None of that matters to her at this point."

"No. I forbid it."

"You have no authority over Evelyn."

"If your uncle and cousin will not see fit to protect her from the likes of Worthington, then I will."

"Uncle Theo invited Worthington here for the very purpose of snagging his attention for one of us. Also, he is a friend to Lucas."

"Charlie, just because a man is friends with another man, does not mean that they are worthy enough to be married to any of their relations."

"You speak nonsense. Your ramblings are those of a jealous man." Charlie paused. The full implication of her statement hitting her. "Do you care for Evelyn in that nature?"

All Sinclair needed to do was to answer in the positive. It would scare Charlotte away and also give him leeway on disrupting Worthington's game. But when he stared at the pool of tears collecting in Charlie's eyes, he refused to answer yes. Because to do so would be a lie that he could never walk away from. He wouldn't hurt Charlotte that way.

When Sinclair didn't answer Charlie, his silence was answer enough. She felt like he'd punched her in the gut. She didn't know how she walked past him without him stopping her. In her daze, she passed Worthington. When he inquired after her, Charlie continued on to her bedroom. Upon reaching the bedroom, Evelyn stood waiting near the window, bouncing on the heels of her feet in excitement. However, one glance at Charlie and her happiness turned to concern. She held her arms open and Charlie ran into them, bawling like a baby.

Sinclair followed behind Charlie to make sure that she made it to the house safely. Worthington tried to stop her, but Charlie blew past him without a second glance. Sinclair laughed when Worthington looked put off by Charlie's disinterest. Worthington looked at where Charlie had come from and encountered Sinclair. Sinclair nodded, and this time he was the one who held the smile of victory. For their best interest, Sinclair would make sure Worthington lost interest in Evelyn and Charlotte.

Especially Charlotte.

Chapter Eight

Sinclair leaned against the fireplace mantle, waiting for Lady Forrester to announce the afternoon's activity. He'd decided overnight if he were to protect the twins, then he would need to be present at all times. Not that he could do much today anyway with the relentless rain falling all morning and into the afternoon. A bevy of suitors surrounded the twins, with Worthington amongst the crowd trying to stake his claim on Charlotte. However, she kept directing him to talk with Evelyn while she flirted with Kincaid and Ralston. Another two gentlemen who weren't worthy of her attentions. No man in this room was, himself included.

During his perusal, he noticed Worthington ignored Evelyn's every attempt to draw him into a conversation. The dejected look upon Evelyn's face frustrated Sinclair. Worthington kept trying to separate Charlotte from the group. Evelyn placed a hand on his sleeve, and Worthington paused in confusion. Evelyn quickly drew her hand away and offered an apology. Then Worthington started talking with Evelyn. The happiness from the earl's attention brightened Evelyn's face. This brought forth another scowl from Sinclair.

Sinclair searched the room until he found the person he needed to speak with. Sinclair saw her talking to Abigail near the windows. The only one who could talk any sense into her sisters was Jacqueline. If she wouldn't see reason about their deception, then he would take the matter to Gray and the duke. For now, he would persuade Jacqueline to stop Charlotte and Evelyn's antics. After Abigail wandered away, Sinclair approached Jacqueline.

"I would say it to be a dreary day, but surrounded by such delightful company, it is far from gloomy."

Jacqueline turned from staring out the window. "Such flattery, Lord Sinclair, could only mean one thing. What is your complaint toward Charlie this time?"

Sinclair laughed. "You wound me, Jacqueline. Can I not pay a compliment to spending time with you?"

"We spend too much time together regularly for this to be a rare occasion of seeing one another. While I value our friendship, I also recognize the tone of your voice when you wish to discuss my sister."

Sinclair sighed. "Am I that obvious?"

"Yes. What has Charlie done for you to seek me out?"

"This concerns Charlotte *and* Evelyn."

"*Charlotte*? This is serious." Jacqueline teased while trying to hold back a smile.

The seriousness of Sinclair amused Jacqueline. Jasper Sinclair was as wild as they came. His antics raised as many brows as Charlotte's did. Charlie and Sinclair's competitiveness was known by all. At any opportunity Sinclair would push Charlotte into her reckless behavior. If she succeeded he would praise her, if Charlie failed, Sinclair's teasing was relentless. Over the last few months, Jacqueline had noted the shift in their relationship. She wondered if Charlotte and Sinclair recognized the difference too.

"Are you aware of your sisters switching identities throughout this house party?" Sinclair lowered his voice.

"Yes." Jacqueline lowered her voice too.

Sinclair stared in shock at her admission. "Why are you not stopping them?"

"Because so far it has been harmless."

"That you are aware of."

"Is there something you wish to confess, Lord Sinclair?" Jacqueline asked in her mother hen tone.

Sinclair winced. He had walked into a trap. With only wanting to make Jacqueline aware of their deceit, he had opened himself into being interrogated. If he weren't careful, Jacqueline would have him confessing to the slight indiscretion he'd shared with Charlie. Then he would find himself *really* trapped. Trapped with a most infuriating, annoying menace who drove him crazy. He glanced over to Charlie and watched her animated face tell a story. Crazy with desire. At that moment Sinclair faced a reality—Charlie had trapped him in her web.

"No. I only plead with you to have them stop this nonsense. One of them will get hurt."

"Which one?"

"Excuse me?"

"Which one will get hurt? Evelyn or Charlotte?"

"I do not know which one."

"I disagree. Take a look at Evelyn over there. Her confidence has blossomed this week. True, a large part of that is due to her impersonation of Charlotte. However, now she is herself and conversing with a gentleman. Before, Evelyn would have been too shy to have stepped out of her shell. So no, I will not discourage their activity for now."

Sinclair scoffed, "Worthington is no gentleman."

"I have seen no proof to refute that."

"You do not know of him as I do, my lady."

"As I do not know of your behavior while not in my presence. But that does not stop me from calling you my friend."

"Point taken."

"I should rephrase my question and ask, is it your intention to hurt Charlotte?"

"Not if I can help it."

"But you have already, have you not?"

Sinclair stayed silent. He wouldn't lie to Jacqueline. He realized his actions from the previous night upset Charlotte. Hell, he was furious with himself for his callous disregard to her feelings, his jealously, and his threats. Most importantly, he was a fool for not kissing her. He'd suffered another sleepless night dreaming about her.

"I overheard Charlotte crying to Evelyn over you."

"I owe Charlotte an apology over my boorish behavior. Nothing happened last night, I promise. I only threatened to tell Worthington and your uncle of their deception."

"And will you?"

"No, not for now, unless I deem it necessary."

"Thank you, Jasper, for understanding. I only wish happiness for my sisters. They are an excellent judge of character, and whoever they choose, it will be because their hearts told them so. I only hope the gentlemen Charlotte and Evelyn gift their hearts to are worthy of them."

Jacqueline squeezed his arm before walking away, leaving Sinclair to wonder if Jacqueline spoke of him. Was he worthy enough for Charlotte? He continued staring at Charlotte. When she glanced his way, he held her gaze searching for an answer. When she granted him a timid smile, he found it. He might not be worthy enough, but he would prove himself every day to win a chance at her heart.

Charlotte had felt Sinclair's stare upon her throughout the day. Even now while he talked to Jacqueline, his stare never wavered. She didn't know what to take of his serious regard. He had made himself more than clear in the stables on what his intentions were. Did he inform Jacqueline of his knowledge of Evelyn and hers deception? If so, Jacqueline only found humor in the situation, if her laughter was anything to judge by.

After Jacqueline left his side, he gazed at Charlotte with a question in his eyes. When she offered him a smile, it seemed to satisfy him. Even though he didn't return her smile or nod her way, he appeared more relaxed. His face lost its seriousness and his fingers no longer clenched the glass he held. When he turned toward the windows his shoulders no longer looked tensed underneath his jacket.

Charlotte longed to go to Sinclair's side. Instead, she stayed talking with the gentlemen surrounding her. They were pleasant enough, but they lacked the energy she always felt around Sinclair. Then there was the matter of Lord Worthington's attention. The earl kept confusing her with Evelyn. Worthington thought his infatuation lay with Charlotte, but it was Evelyn who had portrayed herself *as* Charlotte and he'd believed it. Now that Evelyn acted as herself, Worthington avoided Evelyn and kept trying to draw Charlie away. Charlotte tried to brush his attentions to the side, but he kept persisting. Finally, Evelyn captured his attention with a simple touch. After that, Worthington focused his attention on Evelyn. Which was an immense relief.

Still, Charlotte wanted to seek Sinclair's attention, but she held herself back. Aunt Susanna said never to chase a gentleman. Make them chase you. If you chase them, then you made the work of winning your hand too easy. They must prove they are worthy of your love. But Charlie feared that if she didn't chase Sinclair, he would never realize the love she held for him.

Before Charlotte made her excuses, the parlor door swung open. Oakes, the butler, opened his mouth to announce the visitor when the guest blew past him inside. He shook the rain off his coat, and he winked at the guests.

"A right bloody day. I bet this ruined your plans, Mother."

"Duncan," Charlie squealed, running to his side.

Charlie threw herself in Duncan's arms. Duncan was Aunt Susanna's son. With Duncan here, they would have an ally. Sinclair wanted to reveal their deception, but Duncan would help them. He always played her cohort in her exploits. Duncan wrapped Charlie in his arms, swinging her around.

"Charlie, my girl. You are a sight for sore eyes." Duncan pulled back and looked her over, noticing the blush lighting her cheeks, the ribbons in her hair, and the lovely gown she wore. He waggled his eyebrows and whispered loudly enough for everyone to hear, "A very delectable sight."

Charlie slapped him on the chest and laughed. However, he never let her go, keeping her close to his side while he made his greetings to the party. His mother exclaimed delight that he'd joined the party and informed him he made the perfect number for the next activity they were about to begin. After his entrance died away and everyone resumed their conversations, Duncan drew Charlie to the side.

"That was quite the greeting, cousin."

"I was excited to see you. Aunt Susanna never mentioned you were coming."

"Yes, well, I changed my mind at the last minute. I grew bored at home and thought I would rescue you from your own boredom."

"Bored, or more like escaping from a clinging conquest?"

"Ah, you know me so well. Speaking of conquests, I notice you had a bevy of your own surrounding you when I arrived."

"Yes, well …"

"Mmm, I sense a story that you want to confess. Does your story also explain why Jasper Sinclair is shooting daggers in my direction?"

Charlotte glanced towards Sinclair, catching his glare. Duncan removed his coat, handing it to Oakes, and Charlotte smoothed out his lapel.

"Perhaps."

Duncan chuckled, grasping her hand in his and bringing it toward his mouth. He placed a kiss across her knuckles.

"I cannot wait to hear. Now, before I am reprimanded for my forward behavior, when and where do you want to meet?"

"The usual destination at midnight."

"Would you like me to bring the usual provisions?"

Charlie smirked. "Of course."

"Until later, dear cousin," Duncan whispered in Charlotte's ear.

Duncan sauntered away, clasping Lucas's hand in a handshake when he approached him. When Duncan tried to greet Selina, she turned her head in disapproval, biting out a welcome. Charlotte laughed. While Duncan could charm the very devil, he couldn't break the ice of Selina Pemberton. Selina thought Duncan was a barbaric Scot, too unrefined for her company. However, he was Lucas's cousin and Selina couldn't snub him, even though she wanted to.

Aunt Susanna clapped her hands, drawing everyone's attention. Charlotte wandered over to stand next to Evelyn. Evelyn smiled to Charlie of her happiness. Charlotte grabbed her hand, squeezing her support.

"Now, since this dreadful rain has ruined my plans for an outside scavenger hunt, it has not prevented us from having one. With the help of the servants, we have hidden the items throughout the house. After I pair you ladies with your partners, please grab a basket and the list of items you must search for." Aunt Susanna paused.

"The other afternoon I paired the twins with Worthington and Sinclair. This time, Evelyn, you will be with Lord Worthington, and Charlotte you will have Lord Sinclair for a partner. Only this time, Lord Sinclair, please do not leave Charlotte on her own like you did Evelyn."

Sinclair quietly accepted the reprimand.

Aunt Susanna partnered Jacqueline with Kincaid, and Gemma paired with Lord Ralston. The other guests she randomly matched. When it came to the final four guests, she shocked everyone by matching Lucas with Abigail. Which left Selina to scavenger hunt with Duncan. Charlotte covered her mouth to stifle a giggle at the look on Selina's face. Duncan took great delight in the lady's misfortune by telling her how lucky he was to have her for a partner. Selina couldn't protest the pairing without causing a scene. Duncan winked at Charlotte and she shook her head at his silliness.

"Now, before we begin, there are a set of rules you must follow. You have two hours to return with the items on the list and there must be no cheating. You cannot ask the servants for help. The winners will win the opening waltz at the ball on Saturday. Good luck, ladies and gentlemen."

Chapter Nine

They had been looking for the items on the list for a while now, and Jasper had yet to speak to Charlotte. He had grabbed the list out of Charlotte's hands, scanned it, then handed the paper back. He stalked away in the opposite direction of the others, and Charlotte tried keeping up with his long strides. She rattled on about where they might find some of the items, but Jasper ignored her, taking them deeper into the house where they wouldn't find anything.

"Jasper, slow down. We are not playing a trick on you this time. 'Tis me, Charlotte."

Jasper swung around, backing Charlotte against the wall. His body vibrated with anger, wrapping her in its ferocity.

"I know who you are. I am not like those other dim-witted fools. Believe me, I know you are Charlotte."

"How can you tell the difference?"

"Besides knowing you your entire life?" Charlotte nodded. "Because your eyes flash with fire when you're angry. They soften to the palest green when you're sad. But it is when they turn the darkest, darkest green I really know who you are."

"But Evelyn's eyes do the same."

"Not like yours." Jasper trailed a finger down her cheek.

"Nonsense."

"Mmm." His path continued down her throat. "At this very instance they are changing to the darkest green."

"So that proves to you I am Charlotte?"

"Yes."

"How so?"

"Because, my dear, your eyes are begging me to kiss your lips."

"Utter nonsense," Charlotte sighed, as Jasper brushed his lips across hers.

Jasper couldn't help himself. His jealously fueled the desire to stake his claim on her. To let Charlotte understand that he meant to pursue her. Before Duncan Forrester arrived and Charlotte clung to the earl's side, he'd been about to approach her to apologize for his behavior. But when she greeted Duncan like a long-lost love, he wanted to slug the man. When Lady Forrester paired him with Charlotte, he'd tried to calm his temper, but the wink Duncan sent Charlotte and her giggle only angered Jasper more.

Jasper had intended to find them a room for privacy and forget the game. He wanted to confront Charlotte on her behavior and discover how deeply she was involved with Forrester. But when Charlotte's eyes darkened at his touch, all he wanted to do was to taste her.

One brush across her lips wasn't enough. He desired to savor her lips for an endless amount of time. Jasper slid his tongue inside her mouth, stroking it along hers. With each touch, she responded. Jasper growled and pulled her into his arms. Charlotte slid her hands around his neck, fingers sinking into his hair, pulling his head closer. Their mouths pressed to each other, desperate to quench their thirst.

Charlotte clung to Jasper, his kisses stealing her sanity away. Each time they parted to draw a breath, their lips would lock again. Whenever Jasper kissed her, he overtook her senses, where the only thing Charlotte wanted was him. Ever since this house party started, Jasper had been hot and cold with her. She no longer knew where she stood with him. At this moment, the heat overwhelmed her. She only wanted more. But more would never be enough with Jasper Sinclair.

Jasper pulled away, brushing his thumb across Charlotte's lips. Charlotte's eyes fluttered open.

"That, my dear, is how I know you are Charlotte. Charlotte makes the very air whoosh from my lungs. Charlotte makes me want to kiss her senseless. Charlotte makes me want to shower her with affections." Jasper paused, lowering his head to whisper in her ear. "Charlotte makes me want to lay her on my bed and worship her body with kisses before making her mine."

"Oh my."

Jasper would have laughed at the affect his words had on Charlotte if he weren't so consumed with such conflicting emotions. As from before, Charlotte's kisses overtook all rational thought. His only clear thought was his need for her. Even though holding her in his arms Charlotte's body displayed her desire for him, Jasper's jealously over Forrester stayed forefront in his mind.

He reached behind her and turned the knob on the door. Jasper looked inside and noted the storage room. He urged Charlotte inside and closed the door. The door held no lock. He stepped away and located an old chair, propping it under the knob. Jasper wanted a few moments alone with Charlotte with no interruptions. After he'd had a few questions cleared and he'd stated his intentions toward Charlotte, they would resume the scavenger hunt.

Glancing around, he saw unused furniture covered in sheets. The servants had drawn the drapes to keep the sun from fading the woodwork.

An old table sat in the corner with crates of dishes and candlesticks. Oriental rugs were rolled up and leaning against the wall. He walked over to a couch and took off the cloth covering it.

Charlotte stood next to the door, her eyes darting everywhere but at him. He wanted to put her at ease. Walking to her side, he offered his arm. Jasper escorted Charlotte to the settee and stepped back. He paced one length of the room before he blurted out.

"Are you in love with Duncan Forrester?"

Charlotte's laughter only made him pace again. She never answered him, the laughter growing uncontrollable. Her body tilted, while she clutched at her sides. Jasper frowned at her.

Charlotte couldn't help herself. Jasper's question was ridiculous. Duncan and her? No, Duncan was her brother-in-arms. Was Jasper jealous of Duncan's attention when he arrived? Did their attraction to each other confuse Jasper as much as it did her?

"Well, are you?" Jasper demanded, standing in front of her with his hands clenched in fists at his side.

Charlotte took pity on him. She reached out, wrapping her hands around one of his fists, prying his fingers loose. Her fingers stroked his to lay flat against her palm.

"No, Jasper, I am not in love with Duncan. At least, not in the way you think."

"Yet, you love him?"

"Yes, but only as a cousin or a brother. Nothing more."

Charlotte intertwined their fingers and smiled at him. Jasper breathed a sigh of relief. As he replayed Charlie's greeting to Duncan, he saw it for what it was. Brotherly affection.

Charlie tugged on Jasper's hand, bringing him closer. Jasper sat down next to her. Charlie shouldn't be so bold, but she wanted to kiss Jasper now more than anything. She leaned over and brushed her lips against his.

"Charlie, we must talk."

"Shh, in a minute."

She only wanted one little taste before Jasper got all serious on them. She wanted him reckless, drawing her deeper into his passion. Charlie wanted Jasper to unravel under her touch.

She slid her tongue across his lips. Slowly back and forth, then inside, tasting Jasper. He sat still, returning her kiss, but letting her take control. Her strokes grew bolder, staking her need. With each groan from Jasper, Charlie's doubts of inexperience evaporated. She followed her instincts instead. Her hands stroked along his chest, her fingers slipping his buttons undone. Charlie's hand slipped inside his shirt, her fingers trailing over his firm chest, sliding lower. She wanted to touch more of him.

Charlie's touch drove Jasper wild. Her innocent exploration only heightened his need. He needed to stop this before it got any further out of hand than it already was. But her kisses were too delicious, and not to mention what the soft stroke of her hand did to him. If Charlie slid her hand any lower, she would find out for herself. When her hand moved past his stomach and her fingers slid inside the placket of his trousers, Jasper pulled back, grasping her hands.

"Charlie, this is madness."

"Is it?" she whispered.

Jasper looked at Charlie lying sprawled across the settee while he rose above her. Her cheeks were a light pink, her lips plump from their kisses, and her hair lay in disarray from his hands. He hadn't even realized he ran his fingers through her hair, so lost in their passion. While her dress was still intact, it showed the wrinkles from his hold. His eyes trailed the length of her, noting the effect of his touch. Before he stopped himself, he brushed his thumb across a hardened nipple straining against the dress. Jasper raised his gaze, taking in Charlie's fluttered lashes. Not once did her eyes close; instead the emerald depths stared back boldly asking for him to continue.

"Yes," Jasper groaned.

His mouth devoured her, drawing out the madness. His hand slid inside her dress to stroke the bud between his fingers. Jasper removed his hand and unbuttoned her dress. He slid it off Charlie's shoulders, pooling it around her waist. Her linen chemise was held with thin straps that came off her shoulders without the support of the dress. Charlie watched him in anticipation and he didn't make her wait long.

Jasper lowered the chemise, displaying her breasts. The pale globes beckoned him closer. The rosy tips begged for his mouth. Jasper no longer thought of their need to talk, or to make sense of this madness. His only thought was how to please the woman underneath him. His lips trailed a blaze down Charlie's neck to settle between her breasts. Jasper caressed them, his fingers tracing the contours of Charlie. When his tongue traced lightly over the pebbles, Charlie moaned. Charlie's fingers slid into his hair as he drew a bud into his mouth and sucked softly. He sucked harder, and Charlie gripped his head to her breasts. Jasper had held no clue to his starvation for this woman. But now that Jasper realized the impact she had, he would no longer deny himself.

Jasper pulled Charlie underneath him, laying them the length of the settee. She slid his jacket off his shoulders, untying the cravat. The silk fell from her fingers when Jasper's teeth scraped across her nipples. Charlie arched her back, her body begging for Jasper's devotion. Charlie never imagined a man could make her feel so free, so uninhibited. For that man to be Jasper only heightened her senses. He was the only man who ever pushed her past her safety net. It was only fitting that he would be the man to make her fly. When his hand traveled up her legs and his finger slid up and down her closed thighs, Charlie's curiosity got the better of her. She spread her legs open, welcoming his touch.

His heat consumed her when his touch became bolder. Jasper swept his thumb across her core, settling against her clit. Slowly brushing back and forth, building an ache inside Charlie. When he slid a finger inside her, his mouth clenched on her nipple again. Charlie felt her body floating at the divine sensation. She opened her legs wider, sinking into the pleasure.

Charlie was softness, strong, wantonness, innocence all rolled into one amazing lady. Her curiosity from the pleasure he showed her allowed her to be free with her body. Yet, it was her inexperience that turned Jasper from a gentleman into a man possessed.

Jasper sunk his fingers into her wetness, while his mouth loved her breasts. He slid another finger into her tightness. Her pussy gripped him while he slid them in and out, her wetness clinging. Her moans were music to Jasper's ears, soothing his jealous anger. Jasper pulled his mouth away from her breasts, watching his fingers slide in and out of her fiery core. He only wanted to savor her sweetness. Then he would stop this madness.

When he lowered his head, Charlie asked, "Jasper?"

He didn't answer her. Instead, he placed a soft kiss on her wetness, his tongue tracing a path back and forth. Only one treat would not do. He hungered for the full course of Charlotte Holbrooke. His fingers drove in and out as his mouth consumed Charlie's heat.

He heard Charlie mutter, "Yes, madness."

She had no idea, but Jasper planned to show her. His mouth was relentless on bringing her to the brink of their madness. When his tongue lingered on her clit with forceful strokes, he felt her unraveling around him. Jasper drew his fingers away, replacing them with his tongue. Charlie's hands drifted down to his head, holding him to her. He pressed his tongue in deeper as her hips swayed into him. With a flick of his tongue, Charlie came undone. He raised his head to watch her give herself to him. Her gaze never wavered. He saw every emotion. Pleasure. Desire. Need. Love. That last emotion should scare him. However, it didn't.

Her fingers drifted to his lips. He kissed them and rose to place a softer kiss upon her lips. Her lips clung to his as he slowly drew the kiss out. Jasper gathered Charlie in his arms and held her. Neither one of them spoke. The reason for bringing Charlie into the room, forgotten. He wished to spend the afternoon in each other's arms. Jasper flirted with the danger of them being caught. Their absence wouldn't go unnoticed.

Jasper pulled away and started putting Charlotte's dress back into place. Once she sat before him looking like an innocent debutante, he slid his clothes back together. Charlotte tilted her head, giving him a questioning look that he didn't know how to answer. He moved to the mirror propped against the wall. With a few quick flicks, he made his cravat presentable. He stalled, messing with his clothes.

Charlie would expect a declaration of some sort. One he wasn't ready to make. His feelings toward the minx had changed. But he still didn't understand the emotions she brought forth. Jasper jumped when her palm rested on his shoulder. He hadn't heard her coming closer.

"Jasper?"

Before he could answer Charlie, the doorknob rattled. Charlie's eyes jumped to his. He placed his fingers to her mouth for silence. Then he moved and pressed his body against the door. The voices in the hallway broke out in an argument.

"Selina, my lass, come away from the door. It is time we met the others in the parlor, the game is about over."

"I am not your lass," Selina gritted between her teeth.

"Not for now, at least."

"Not now or ever."

"Ah, ever is such a long time. I love myself a challenge, though."

"You barbarian Scot, I am your cousin's betrothed."

"A minor issue to overcome."

"Does your lust have no bounds? When you first arrived, your possessive display toward *Charlotte Holbrooke* shocked the room," Selina sneered.

"No need to be jealous, lass. You hold my heart. Now come away from the door, so we can join the rest of the party."

"I am not jealous, you fool. I only want to prove how little miss innocent Charlotte is not as innocent as she portrays. Sinclair snuck her away into this room. Probably for a secret tryst. What is even more hilarious is that, he plays with both sisters. I saw him sneak away with Evelyn into the woods during the pall-mall game. When she returned with her hair mussed, he was nowhere to be found."

"You are a vindictive shrew, Selina Pemberton, to take pleasure from other's misfortunes."

The knob rattled with more force and the door shook. Charlie stared wide-eyed at Jasper while he tried barring Selina's entrance. Charlie had thought they had been careful and no one realized their indiscretions. If Selina spread any rumors, would anyone believe her? If not, who else had seen them alone?

"Let me go, you Scottish heathen."

As quickly as their time was interrupted, silence descended on them. Charlie moved to come closer to the door, but Jasper held up a hand to stop her. She paused, waiting. Then through the closed panel they listened to a resounding slap.

"How dare you?" Selina screeched.

Then the only sounds were of Selina's footsteps stomping away. A loud chuckle echoed from the hallway. Duncan knocked, letting them know it was safe to come out, then he spoke to them through the door.

"I am going to turn a blind eye to the fact you are alone in the room with Charlie, Sinclair. If you do not make right by her, I will make sure you do. Charlie, my girl, you owe me a favor. On the other hand, I might owe you."

They listened to Duncan walk away. Charlie turned to the mirror that Jasper had used. She fussed with her hair. Duncan's threat hung heavy between them. Charlie didn't want Jasper forced into anything he didn't want to be regarding her. She wanted him to choose her and make a grand gesture. They had to return to the others before Selina sent a search party after them. When she turned around, Jasper waited by the door. He had moved the chair away and was waiting for them to leave. Charlie picked up the basket with the list. She glanced at the list and knew where to locate some of the items quickly.

"Charlie, we need to talk."

She nodded.

"Will you meet me tonight at midnight at your special spot?"

Charlie was about to nod when she remembered she promised to meet Duncan there at the same time. She couldn't call off Duncan, he would be too suspicious. If Duncan found out she was meeting Sinclair instead, he would attempt to protect her virtue. She didn't want the men to have a confrontation.

"I cannot get away then. Can we meet at dawn for a ride? None of the guests will rise that early."

"I shall await your company with much impatience." Jasper brushed a tendril of hair away from her face. "I am not playing you false, Charlotte. I aim to prove it to you."

Charlotte nodded, stepping away from him. Jasper's touch invoked too many desires. She needed to part from him before she threw herself at him again. Charlotte was not safe alone in the company of Jasper Sinclair. Their attraction sizzled between them, causing Charlotte to abandon all rational thought.

Jasper noticed Charlotte's nervousness and mistook it for embarrassment at almost getting caught. He wanted to ease her fears, but knew their time was limited before someone found them. Jasper cracked open the door and noted the empty hallway before ushering Charlotte out. She held the list up and took off. The only thing Jasper could do was to follow her. She impressed him by finding a few items quickly, filling their basket. Soon they heard the tinkling of the bell, signaling the end of the game. Jasper continued to follow Charlotte at a discreet distance, not wanting to cause any gossip.

When they entered the parlor, Charlotte glanced over her shoulder offering him a shy smile. A blush spread gracefully across her cheeks. She hurried over to her sisters and friends, laughing at them over the game. He stood there smiling like a besotted fool. Jasper turned to leave the room and ran into Charlie's uncle and Forrester. Forrester glared at him, reinstating his threat. However, the Duke of Colebourne gave him a smile of approval. Did Forrester tell the old man of his suspicions?

Chapter Ten

Charlie snuck out of the house into the darkness, heading to her secret destination. She had promised Evelyn she would be careful and assured her that no one would discover her missing. Charlie risked getting caught, especially since the house had not quieted yet for the night. The ladies had taken themselves to their bedrooms, but the gentlemen decided on a late night game of cards and billiards. Uncle Theo's entertainment room was grand enough for a billiards table and some gaming tables. Before she slipped out of the house, she heard the gentlemen's raucous laughter and saw the billow of smoke floating out of the room. Their loudness could only be due to the amount of spirits consumed. After dinner, while they waited for the gentlemen to join them, Aunt Susanna made the comment of the gentlemen growing bored with country life to her elderly companions. Then one of the other ladies made a comment about sowing wild oats. A confusing comment Charlie would ask Duncan to explain once they met up.

Once Charlie reached her destination, she swung on the low branch and made her way up a few more. Leaning against the base of the tree, she brought one leg up under her chin, while the other swung lazily back and forth. She looked toward the house and noted the many windows with lights ablaze. It would appear the gentlemen were not the only restless ones. Charlie wondered what Jasper was doing right now. Did he join the gentlemen for a night of relaxation? Or did he lie in bed? Did he think of her as she was of him? Throughout dinner, he'd occupied her thoughts with every glance. She didn't even remember who she sat and talked with during the meal. Even now she couldn't stop thinking about him and imagining what other delights he'd pleasure her with.

"Charlie, my girl, are you going to join me or sit in the tree all night gawking at the house?"

"I am not gawking."

"I have set out our midnight rendezvous in splendor delight and you never moved a muscle."

Charlie looked below to see Duncan relaxed on the blanket with the rations of treats he stole from the kitchen. He grabbed a grape and popped it into his mouth. How did she not hear him arrive? Charlie climbed down the tree, jumping off from the lowest branch. Her jump landed wrong, and she rolled onto the blanket, laughing at her mishap.

"It must be the dress-wearing that has you off your game."

"Hush." Charlie swatted at Duncan before grabbing a piece of cheese. "You know your mama forces me to wear them. Also, I will not embarrass Uncle Theo in front of his guests."

"Well then, I hope you do not run into any guests on your return. Some of those uptight prudes might not understand your current state of dress."

Charlie looked down at the trousers and loose white cotton shirt she pulled on. It was her usual attire when she visited the stables and one she always wore when she wandered the estate. It was the only way she'd climbed the tree so easily. They were the only garments that made her comfortable enough to be her true self. Plus, they were a lot less confining. She wasn't all trussed up on display.

Charlie dug into the treats Duncan brought. She was starving, since she didn't eat much at dinner. Jasper's unwavering stare had unsettled her. Her anticipation for the morning to arrive to spend time alone with him grew. Would he kiss her again? Charlie hoped so.

"I will sneak in through the servants' quarters. No one will know the difference, especially when I wear this." Charlie threw her hat at Duncan.

Duncan laughed at her disguise. They soon settled into their regular discussion. Duncan told her of the widow he'd escaped from in Edinburgh. His tale had her in stitches. When he described how the widow waited naked for him in his study, shocking his servants, Charlie's laughter filled the night air.

"Duncan Forrester, you are one naughty Scot."

"One you want to be naughty with?" He waggled his eyebrows at Charlie.

Charlie's laughter died away. She felt the heat of a blush covering her face. Charlie was thankful for the darkness. The light of the moon wasn't bright enough to display her blush. If so, Duncan's teasing would never stop. She broke the chocolate biscuits into crumbs. The awkward silence filled the night air. Duncan pulled the biscuit from her hands.

"I stole your favorite treat for you to eat, not to destroy," Duncan teased, handing her another biscuit.

"Thank you," Charlie mumbled, taking a bite. The savory chocolate exploded in her mouth. She moaned at the exquisite taste. Cook had the skill to make chocolate biscuits melt in one's mouth.

"Oh, to be on the end of that moan."

"Stop it, Duncan."

"Not until you tell me why you were flirting with those blokes when I arrived and what you were doing alone with Jasper Sinclair in the storage room this afternoon. Because any other time, my flirtatious attitude never bothered you. In fact, if I remember correctly, you used to flirt back to inflate my ego."

"That was before."

"Before what, my girl?"

"Before Uncle Theo threw this maddening matchmaking house party. Before Evelyn convinced me to help her. Before Jasper Sinclair kissed me." Charlie ended on a sigh.

"While I would love to focus on Sinclair's untoward behavior, we better start at the beginning."

"'Tis a long story."

Duncan leaned back, folding his arms behind his head. "I have all night. Do you have somewhere to be?"

"Not until dawn."

"Should I ask where?"

"No, it is part of my story."

"I wait in anticipation then."

Charlie laughed. "Why is life so confusing?"

"Because if it weren't, it would be too boring. Boring does not work for people like you and me. We thrive on adventure, complexity, curiosity."

"Perhaps we are just foolish."

"Mmm, perhaps. Now why do you believe Uncle Theo is using this house party in a matchmaking attempt?"

"Because I overheard Lucas and him discussing the matter. He wants to see us settled before anything happens to him. Whoever does not make a match from the party will travel to London for the upcoming season."

"That will be mighty pricey."

"Yes, Lucas agrees. However, Uncle thinks the gentlemen he invited would be perfect matches. Uncle Theo and your mother have been throwing us in their clutches at every opportunity they can."

"I wondered why Mother was insistent on me not joining the festivities. She forbade me to come. When I questioned her, she gave me a silly excuse that Uncle Theo invited his old friends to the house party. The reason for her visit was to chaperone and to keep you girls out of their way. Imagine my delight to see a roomful of young debutantes ripe for plucking."

"Exactly why your mother dissuaded you from coming, my friend."

"All right, which explains the party. Now onto Evelyn. What does she need help with?"

"The reason is complicated."

"Spill."

"If I do, you must promise that you will take no action against the gentleman it involves. It is pertinent that you keep your silence. Do you promise?"

"I will only keep the promise until at any time the said gentleman we plan on discussing does not stand up to his advances."

Duncan would protect any of them if someone behaved wrongly against them. She would betray Evelyn on her secret, only because they were running out of time. If Worthington didn't fall in love with Evelyn before the ball ended on Saturday night, Charlie didn't think her sister would have another chance.

Charlie had heard Aunt Susanna and her cronies gossiping yesterday. Worthington needed a bride, and soon. When his father passed away, he'd left his family destitute. Worthington sunk his available funds into his breeding program. The banks held the mortgages on his homes that weren't entailed. The creditors were on the brink of closing his accounts. With a mother, three younger sisters and a brother, he needed the dowry of a bride to help dig him out of his misfortune. If he didn't find a bride at the party, then he would return to London and seek any eligible debutante or heiress for his agenda. By the time they would reach London, he would have already secured himself a bride, and Evelyn would forever lose her chance at love and happiness. She didn't tell Evelyn of this latest news, because it would only have discouraged her. Perhaps Duncan could help them make Worthington fall for Evelyn.

"Evelyn has fallen in love with Worthington. At an earlier visit, they had a moment that endeared her heart to him."

"What kind of moment?"

"A scandalous one." Charlie winced.

"My promise is slowly disappearing," Duncan warned.

"Please try to understand. After their time together, Evelyn came away in love. The only hitch is that Worthington thinks he seduced *me*. When he spoke my name, Evelyn didn't correct him."

"Not only is Evelyn's reputation in jeopardy, so is yours."

"Yes. Except we have been switching identities throughout the party. Each time your mother pairs me with Worthington, Evelyn takes my place. You should see her transformation. She has come out of her shell and glows. She *glows*, Duncan. I have not seen her this alive since Mama and Papa were alive."

"All right, I will keep my promise. How will Evelyn handle Worthington's anger once he learns of her deception? Because he will be furious. His pride already suffers. Your deceit would push him to deny any involvement with Evelyn."

"But by that time he will have fallen in love with Evelyn. Worthington will forgive her for everything."

"Charlie, my girl, it does not work that way. He will be furious for being duped. Also, consider Evelyn. Does she not deserve a man to love her for herself? She will always wonder who his affections lie with. You or her? In the end she could come to resent you."

Charlie listened to Duncan's argument and doubted their plans. They never took into account the fallout of their deception. Evelyn assumed Worthington would fall in love with her. That their attraction would blossom into love. Were they foolish to believe that attraction led to love?

"I have to believe that our plan will work. Why, even today, after Worthington kept trying to grab my attention, Evelyn charmed him to talk to her. Aunt Susanna paired them together for the scavenger hunt, and Evelyn has been overjoyed since."

"I hope for her sake that it works. Now, please tell me why I should not tell Uncle Theo about the two hours you spent alone with Sinclair while you should have been playing in the scavenger hunt?"

"I wish I could explain. I am confused myself on why Sinclair and I have this … this thing."

Duncan rolled over, leaning his head on his hand. "And what exactly is this thing?" he teased.

Charlie moaned and lay down. She stared up at the stars in the sky, wondering how to describe the thing Sinclair and her shared without telling Duncan of their intimacy.

"I do not understand how, but he discovered our deception on the first day. He said there were differences between Evelyn and I."

"He has known you girls your entire life. I am sure after the time you have spent with him at the stables, he can see the differences. Evelyn and you are as different as night and day."

"Maybe."

"Will I need to protect your virtue too after this house party is over, if Sinclair does not offer for your hand in marriage?"

Charlie didn't answer.

"I will take your silence as a yes."

"One minute we are arguing, the next we are in each other's arms, and Jasper is kissing me, making my knees grow weak. His kisses have opened my soul to a whirlwind of emotions I want to explore. He threatened to tell on us, but I do not think he will any longer. We are meeting for a ride at dawn. Jasper wants to spend time with me."

"Not without a chaperone. I will meet you."

"No, please Duncan. Do not make me regret talking with you. I want to spend time alone with Jasper and explore these feelings we have for each other. I promise things will progress no further than what I have allowed."

"And what have you allowed?" Duncan scowled.

"Nothing much. Just a few kisses." Charlie's face was on fire now.

"Charlie, you must understand. While I am your friend, I am also a member of your family whose duty it is to protect your honor."

"I understand, but please just this one time, trust that I will use my best judgment."

"You know I cannot refuse you. I will only give you this one opportunity to be alone with Jasper Sinclair. After your ride, Evelyn and you must promise to drop your deception and bring these gentlemen to terms honestly. And I say gentlemen lightly. I still do not understand why Uncle Theo invited these particular gentlemen to his estate."

"I already told you. He is playing matchmaker."

"Yes, but the gentlemen he invited are rakes and scoundrels. Some of them have reputations full of scandal. Worthington himself is rumored to have at least two mistresses at a time. Sinclair is wild with his money, making obscene bets with his racehorses. And he is no innocent with women either. There is a reason all the widows flock to him. He may not bed them when their husbands are alive, but before they are buried in the ground, you will find Sinclair buried in their wives. I do not mean to be so cruel, my dear. I only want you to understand the kind of man you are risking your heart to love. Is he worth it?"

"Yes."

Charlie's answer was quick and firm. After Sinclair's first kiss, her heart made the decision. There would be no other but him.

"Do you agree to stop your deceit after your ride with Sinclair?"

Charlie rolled over, mimicking Duncan by propping her head on her hand. "If you will answer a couple of my questions."

"All right."

"Can you explain what sowing your wild oats means?"

Duncan choked on the cookie he was eating, sending a few crumbs spluttering in the air.

"Where did you hear that comment from?"

"Aunt Susanna and her cronies when they were describing the gentlemen's boredom."

"Um, the comment means when a gentleman likes to, um, you know."

"No, I do not. That is why I am asking you."

Duncan sighed. "It is when a gentleman likes to keep company with a variety of females in a sexual nature before he takes the long walk down the wedding aisle."

"Oh."

Before Charlie asked any more questions pertaining to the subject, Duncan asked, "And your second question?"

"Why did Selina slap you?"

Instead of answering, Duncan started cleaning up their midnight picnic. His silence intrigued Charlie more. If she didn't know any better, she thought Duncan was blushing. Which was absurd. A grown man blushing over a mere slap. Unless it was more?

"Well?" Charlie probed again when Duncan hadn't answered.

"Nothing. She was just perturbed for my standing in her way. We need to return before someone spots us." Duncan tried pulling the blanket out from beneath Charlie while avoiding her eyes.

It was more than nothing. What would make Duncan so uncomfortable that he would avoid the subject? Especially when they shared everything? Duncan was the closest thing she had to a brother, besides Lucas. There would be only one reason for Duncan to keep a secret. The repercussions he would meet if anyone discovered the truth would be life-defining.

"You kissed Selina," Charlie whispered.

Duncan closed his eyes and hung his head. His shame at kissing his cousin's betrothed revealed itself in his rigid form. There was no explanation for what came over him at that moment. The memory of taking Selina's soft lips under his brought forth another wave of guilt. All he knew was one minute he tried preventing Selina from discovering Charlie and Sinclair, and the next minute he wanted to punish her vindictiveness with his kiss. He didn't understand if he wanted to prove to Selina or himself that she held any emotion for him. And he did. He'd felt her mouth soften under his when he slid his tongue inside. She melted for the briefest of moments before she pulled away and slapped him.

He opened his eyes and nodded at Charlie. Her eyes widened and her mouth dropped open. Duncan would have laughed at her expression if it weren't directed at him. He swore, dragging his hand through his hair. Now Charlie knew his secret and he would need to persuade her to keep her mouth closed. Charlie didn't hide her hatred toward Selina. At any opportunity, Charlie tried to thwart the lass. While he agreed with Charlie that Selina wasn't the woman for Lucas, it was out of their control. Uncle Theo had made that decision long ago. For him to cross that line that was his burden to fix, which he could manage as long as Charlie stayed silent. When Charlie burst out laughing, Duncan knew he was doomed.

"Why on earth would you do that?" Charlie asked between her bouts of laughter.

"Why do you think?" Duncan growled. "I was trying to protect you."

"And that was the only reason?"

Another question that he couldn't answer without telling the truth. He could lie, but Charlie would know. To be honest even with himself over the subject of Selina Pemberton, he didn't quite understand. The lass stirred emotions in him. Selina was off limits, only meant for Lucas. But it hadn't stopped Duncan from imagining what it would feel like to be with her. Her cloud of vulnerability drew her to him. She always portrayed herself as a snobbish debutante who always got what she wanted. But when nobody watched, Selina's demeanor dropped, and she was an insecure, lonely chit wishing the other ladies would include her in their circle. Duncan noticed Selina watching with envy when the other girls gathered together. However, the use of her waspish tongue kept her apart.

"No," Duncan admitted.

For Duncan to admit to wanting to kiss Selina of his own free will was a recipe for disaster. What Charlie didn't understand was why? Selina was a vindictive shrew. She wasn't good enough for Lucas, and definitely not good enough for Duncan. Even if it were possible, they were complete opposites. Selina was a pampered bitch who made life a living hell, while Duncan was a carefree bachelor always seeking the pleasures of life.

"That explains it all now."

"What does, lass?"

"All the men in this family are looney." Charlie laughed.

"If that is the case, it is only because the ladies in this family have made us crazy." Duncan lunged after Charlie to tickle her.

Charlie took off running around the tree, her laughter growing louder. Before Duncan could grab her, she scrambled up the tree, sitting on the low branch. Duncan wouldn't follow for fear of putting too much weight on the limb. The last time he had, he ended up breaking his arm when the branch broke. Charlie had learned a few more curse words that day.

"Come down, Charlie, my girl, before I climb after you."

"And risk another broken arm?"

"It would be worth it to make you squirm."

"No need. Catch me," Charlie shouted before jumping.

Chapter Eleven

Sinclair stepped outside for a breath of fresh air. The billiards room had grown heavy with smoke and drunken gentlemen. Every man in attendance grew bored with the house party's confinement. The rainy weather the last two days made it more unbearable for them. Except for Sinclair. Today had the opposite effect on him. His time alone with Charlotte only made him wish for more rainy days. There were quite a few places to which he wanted to steal her away. He may have joined the other gentlemen tonight for more gentlemanly pursuits, but they weren't what he desired. Sinclair was restless for a chit with luxurious dark tresses, lush green eyes, soft pink lips, and a body that molded to his with perfection. He couldn't steal into her bedroom, because she shared one with Evelyn. His patience would be near the end by the time they met at dawn. Sinclair wished Charlie would have met him tonight. But he understood the risk if they were caught together alone. This afternoon had been too close of a call. He would have done right by her. It just wasn't what he wanted for them. Not once he realized the depth of his feelings for the girl.

Sinclair looked off into the distance to where he wanted to steal away with Charlie. The sight of a lantern glowing shocked him. Did Charlie change her mind, and he didn't receive the message? Was she waiting there now for him to join her? He took off, hoping that she waited. When he drew closer to the tree, he stopped in his tracks. Charlie was at her favorite spot, but she was not alone. No, Charlie shared her company with Forrester. She'd lied to him earlier, claiming … Charlie hadn't given him an excuse to why they couldn't meet, but now he saw why she wouldn't meet him. She had made another set of plans for a midnight rendezvous.

Sinclair drew closer, his steps silent in the grass when he came upon the couple wrapped in an intimate embrace. Forrester stood with Charlie clasped in his arms and her arms wrapped around his neck. They were both laughing. Then their laughter died with Forrester pressing his head against Charlotte's forehead. Sinclair listened to them whispering promises about keeping secrets. Now he understood the full impact of Forrester's glare earlier after he returned Charlie to the parlor.

"Will you keep my secret?" asked Duncan.

"As long as you keep my mine," Charlie whispered.

Sinclair called, "You are the most sought-after lady at this house party, are you not, Charlotte Holbrooke? And here I thought I had won your affections. But it would appear that you have spread them wide. I wonder where Worthington is?" Sinclair glanced around. "Or have you promised to meet him in the stables?"

"Jasper, you misunderstand."

Sinclair turned and walked away. He didn't even want to listen to any excuses. They were all lies. The couple's embrace spoke volumes of their intimate relationship. Charlie made him a fool.

"Duncan, put me down."

Once Duncan set Charlie on her feet, she ran after Jasper. His long strides took him farther away, but Charlie picked up her pace too. She caught him, grasping at his arm. She tried to pull him around, but he shook off her grasp and kept moving toward the house.

"Jasper, please stop. I can explain," Charlie pleaded.

Sinclair stopped, turned around and stormed back to Charlie. She stood panting. He towered above her, his anger held back by a thin thread. While moments earlier the anticipation of their ride consumed his soul, now fury overtook his senses. His need to punish Charlotte for her deception would be what fueled his cruel words.

"There is nothing to explain, my dear girl. I am only letting my sense of competitiveness get the better of me. I am upset that Forrester charmed your innocence away before I had the chance to. Nothing but a little healthy male competition. Since Forrester spoiled you, I will seek my pleasures elsewhere. At least we have our memories from this afternoon. Your sweet samples were divine." Sinclair wagged his eyebrows for effect. "I will keep our little secret on that, no need to anger Forrester," Sinclair finished on a whisper.

Charlotte's stood rooted in disbelief. She wanted to explain why she was alone with Duncan. Charlie thought Jasper would understand, instead he declared his true intentions. She had been nothing but a game. He only pursued her because of a competition amongst the other gentlemen at the house party. She had thought she meant more to him than his usual conquests. But she had been wrong. Jasper had made her feel special. Her time spent with him during the house party gave her confidence as a woman. Tears leaked from her eyes as she stared at the stranger before her. She didn't think Sinclair was capable of this behavior, but his comments spoke otherwise.

Sinclair watched the tears fall from Charlie's eyes. Any other time he would provoke her toward anger. But this time was different. He hardened his heart toward those tears. They were an act, just as was her kiss earlier. It would appear Charlie had wanted to practice her womanly charms during this house party. And he fell into her trap, like the fool he was. No, he wouldn't fall for her tears too, they were only an act to playing the injured female. Another ploy a debutante used to trap a gentleman. His sarcastic laugh filled the air around them. He expected better from Charlie.

Charlie gasped at Sinclair's laughter. It was dark and hurt her as deeply as his words. She took off running toward the house. She wanted away from him, too hurt to explain herself. He didn't want to hear her reasons anyway. Sinclair's anger was more than clear. After she got her emotions under control, she would meet him for their ride and try to explain.

Sinclair watched Charlie run toward the house. While the sensible side of him pushed him to run after her and apologize for his cruelty, the other side pushed him to indifference. However, that side no longer stood strong. Not since he savored the sweetness of Charlie. Not only was he a fool, he was also a cruel bastard for hurting her. He started after Charlie, only to be pulled up short. A hand gripped his neck and Forrester growled in his ear.

"Stay away from the lass, you have done enough damage."

"I could say the same as you. Will you offer for her in the morning?"

"I have no reason to."

"You compromise her where anyone can see. I think that is more than enough reason to offer for her hand."

"You are a fool, Sinclair. If you are so worried about Charlie's reputation, then you ask to marry her. I'm not saddling myself with that lass."

"She deserves better."

"That we agree on, but I am not that bloke."

"I doubt if your uncle and cousin would agree."

"Oh, I believe they would after I inform them of the company she has kept and the activities she has partaken in this week."

"Excluding yourself, of course?" asked Sinclair.

"Of course."

"If you will not make an offer for her hand, then you will not keep me away from her."

"I will, if you continue to confuse and hurt her."

"I am going to issue you the same warning. Stay away from her, Forrester. Charlie is mine."

"We shall see."

Forrester walked away from Sinclair, leaving him before Jasper might punch the smug Scot. While Charlie had lied to him and he caught her in a compromising act, it still didn't extinguish the rush of desire he felt for her. Her vulnerability when he lashed at her weakened him. Sinclair needed to keep his distance though until he figured how he wanted to proceed with Charlie. Maybe if he stayed away, Forrester would see the error of his ways and make good by Charlie. If not, then Sinclair would do everything in his power to make Charlie his.

~~~~~~

Worthington stood hidden behind the bushes, watching the interchange between Sinclair and Forrester. He had followed Sinclair out, wondering where he was off to. Worthington considered Sinclair competition in winning Charlotte Holbrooke's hand. He was as shocked as Sinclair when he witnessed Charlotte in Forrester's arms. Even more shocked when he heard Sinclair declare how they were to meet in private in the morning. He not only had Sinclair to compete with for Charlotte's hand, but also Duncan Forrester. Charlotte's greeting of the Neanderthal earlier in the day sent many to whisper of her loose morals.

He couldn't afford to align himself with someone of that nature, but he'd learned the chit held the rights to the foal about to be born. If he convinced

Charlotte that he held feelings for her, then she would accept his offer of marriage. Then through the dowry he would own the next prized foal to enhance his stables. As it stood now, if he didn't marry well soon, then he would lose the one thing he had worked so hard on all these years. His wastrel of a father destroyed their legacy with his immoral behavior. He needed that horse—and to get the horse he needed Charlotte Holbrooke. She was nothing but a means to an end.

At every opportunity to press his match, he ended up being stuck with her twin sister. The quiet, boring one. Oh, she would be the perfect example for a wife. Evelyn had a virtuous character, she was pleasant to gaze upon, and her manners were impeccable. His mother would love her and she would be an exemplary role model for his brother and sisters. The only thing was, he'd vowed to never betray his wife the way his father betrayed their mother. To never give cause to any rumors of extra-marital behavior outside of their bed chamber. He would be faithful to his wife. While he wanted a biddable wife, he also required one with passion. There was no denying Charlotte Holbrooke contained enough passion to light an explosion. Evelyn Holbrooke, on the other hand, would cause him to fall asleep during the act of lovemaking. The two sisters might be identical in appearances, but their personalities were different as night and day. While one ran hot, the other ran cold.

He'd had a pleasant enough time during the scavenger hunt with Evelyn today. Only because he used it to his advantage to learn more about Charlotte. Even though what Evelyn told him didn't sound quite correct. Not that he paid much attention to her ramblings, he was too distracted wondering why they never crossed paths with Charlotte and Sinclair. It was as if the two of them had disappeared. When they returned to the drawing room, Charlotte looked a little flushed and her dress was pressed with wrinkles. Which only meant one thing. Sinclair compromised the chit. Not only Sinclair, but now Forrester too. The girl played loose with her favors. Once they got married, he would need to make it clear to her they were to stay faithful to one another. He would not be cuckold by her, nor would he obtain a mistress.

Only one other thing confused him about the chit. On occasions they would have this sizzling attraction. He couldn't keep his hands off her. Nor his lips. Her kisses unmanned him. Why just yesterday, he pulled her into a linen closet and explored her feminine wiles. Her touch caressed him like silk. Her soft cries of pleasure sang in his ears. The taste of her lips had him drowning in ecstasy. Her kisses had grown bolder than the innocence of the young miss he seduced last winter. It only made him want to make her his as soon as possible. Then there were the other times, when her touch left him cold. No physical connection or arousal. Did he want to continue to pursue Charlotte knowing that she shared her favors so easily? Yes, he must, for he had a family to support. He would have to overlook her activities for now. Perhaps he could sustain them by involving Gray. Yes, he would tell his friend how loose his cousin's morals were and convince Gray to have a talk with Charlotte. If that didn't work he would plead his case to the duke. He would make Charlotte Holbrooke his, in any way possible. They would work out their differences after they wed.

Chapter Twelve

The pounding of horse's hooves jerked Charlie awake inside the stable. After she had dried her tears and calmed down from Jasper's cruel words, she snuck back outside to wait for him. Jasper would come to the stable, eventually. Not at the time they arranged, but earlier to avoid her. And she had been correct. Charlie peered into the darkness, realizing it wasn't even close to dawn. The moon still shone high in the darkness.

Charlie slipped out of the stall, knowing her way by heart. She had spent her entire life inside these stables and knew every nook and cranny. With her thoughts occupied by Jasper, Charlie ran smack dab into Emery, the stable master, when she rounded the corner. She should have been more alert, since Emery complained loudly about being awakened by an ungrateful marquess in the dead of night.

"Whoa, what mischief are you about, girl?"

"I was checking on Sapphire. I worry with her time so near."

Emery eyed her with suspicion. "You were no consorting with that Sinclair fellow, were you?"

"Noo." Charlie drew out.

"Humph."

"Was the marquess here?"

"Just stormed off like a beehive of bees were after him."

"Where to?"

"How do I know? Said something about a cold swim. Is this party about over? These rich toffs invading the stables are wearing on me nerves."

"But Sinclair is always here."

"Aye, but even he is actin' strange."

"It will be over in a few days, Emery. Why don't you return to your bed?"

"Soon as I see you to the house, your uncle will have my hide for you being in the stables after dark."

"I am not ready to leave Sapphire. Please let me stay. I promise Uncle Theo will never know."

"I am not sure about this, girl."

"Would you allow me to stay for some of cook's chocolate biscuits?"

"The kind with the chunks of chocolate still in them?"

"The very same."

Emery glanced around, making sure Charlie would come to no harm. "Do you promise to sneak back into your bed before dawn?"

"I promise."

"All right then, go to your horse. I am back to bed."

"Thank you, Emery. You are the sweetest." Charlie planted a kiss on Emery's cheek.

The old man blushed. "Off with you," he mumbled, walking back to his cot.

Charlie sat on a stack of hay nearby, waiting long enough for Emery to fall back asleep. When his snores started vibrating off the walls, Charlie snuck outside. It was too risky for her to take a horse. Emery would know it was her and alert Uncle Theo. Thankfully, it was a full moon and the stars still lit up the night sky. She knew where Jasper had ridden to. It was his favorite spot, the pond. It bordered the land where his and Uncle Theo's property met. She took off on foot—unaware that somebody watched her from afar.

~~~~~~~

Jasper sliced through the water as if a sea monster pursued him. But the only monster pursing him was the enormous green one. Jealously was a wasted emotion, but one that consumed him at the moment. Not only jealousy, but anger. Somewhere inside him, shouting for notice, were the emotions of betrayal and hurt. How could Charlie dally with another man after the passion they shared? Her eyes spoke volumes of innocence when he confronted her, but they had to be the ploys of a young lady when caught in a blunder. However, Charlie wasn't your normal lady. She was too straightforward. More like blunt. She never mixed words or actions.

Jasper's strokes slowed, processing what he saw. Yes, Forrester held Charlie in his arms, but they were only laughing. There was no passion exchanged between them. Forrester held Charlie not as a lover but as a friend. If Jasper cleared his vision of the forest in front of his eyes, he would remember the friendly bond Charlie and Forrester held. He had watched them from afar for years, and they had only ever been friendly, never anything more. He owed Charlie an apology. But Forrester, no, the Scot could go to hell as far as Jasper was concerned, for being so cavalier about Charlie's virtue. Even if Forrester had tried to provoke Jasper to make right by his own ruination of Charlie. He had planned to in his own time. Not by the force of a scoundrel who ruined more ladies than he should. Which explained his reason for joining the house party. Forrester probably found some sweet lass and tempted her with promises sprinkled with kisses and rode to the house party to escape her clutches. The bounder.

Jasper rolled over to float on his back, staring at the star-filled night. The flickering objects gave light to the surrounding landscape as if it were daybreak. He knew nobody was about. Few ventured to this pond because of the rocks surrounding it. The exclusion kept him hidden from curious eyes. Jasper had felt comfortable enough to shuck his clothing before diving into the icy cold depths. At the time, the chilliness of the water soothed his fiery temper. Now that he calmed down, the water's temperature prompted him to turn back. He would light a fire to warm himself before riding back and maybe even finish his night sleeping under the stars. Anything to keep him from the stables at dawn. From her. He wasn't ready to face Charlie yet. Just the thought of her warmed his blood again. Jasper flipped over and dove under the water to cool himself again. But no matter how long he stayed in the water it would never cool him enough. Every cell of his body heated because she never left his mind. Charlie consumed his soul.

He broke out of the water, standing waist-deep to lock eyes with the one woman fueling his indecent thoughts. A ripple of water surrounded him, the only movement in the pond. He remained where he stood when his gaze took Charlie in. She sat with her knees pulled up under her chin, his suit coat draped across her shoulders. The night air, while not cold for the spring, held a slight chill. Charlie had never looked more vulnerable as she did now. He had caused that look. Jasper raked his hands through his hair, frustrated at himself. Then there was the matter of being stuck in the water. His blatant disregard of his clothing earlier had not entered his mind to be a problem. But now it was another story. He wanted to wrap Charlie in his arms and kiss her heartache away. Instead he stood in the freezing water, because the shock of his indecency would scare the poor girl away.

Charlie had been watching Jasper swimming, wondering what his thoughts were. The movement of his body mesmerized her. At first he sliced through the water in anger, his strokes swift in the chilly water. Then when he flipped onto his back with the moonlight shining down on him, Charlie held still. She didn't move a muscle in fear he would discover her attention drawn to his manhood. Charlie couldn't tear her gaze away from the strength and vitality of Jasper Sinclair. He was a perfect specimen of a man, from his wet locks to his feet fluttering in the water. Charlie raked her eyes slowly down his form. Jasper appeared at peace with his face relaxed, and his eyes closed. His lips no longer held the disappointment they had earlier. Her eyes trailed over his muscular chest, which had been firm against her breasts. When her eyes dipped lower, following the patch of hair, she glanced away, then returned her stare to focus on how his hardness floated in the water. She imagined how it would feel. The water would help guide her hand along the smooth length. Charlie tore her gaze away and continued traveling down the long length of his legs. His thighs were muscular from the many hours he spent riding horses.

When his body disappeared under the water, Charlie groaned in disappointment. Her lengthy perusal awoke her inner desires. She wanted to gaze upon Jasper all night and into each day following. After seeing Jasper naked before her eyes, Charlie wanted him to make love to her. She wanted to give herself to Jasper. He was the only man for her. There would be no other to ever hold her interest. Or her heart.

As his powerful arms swam through the water again, Charlie only wanted Jasper to hold her in them. To pull her in his embrace and devour her with his mouth. Her body held an ache only Jasper could ease. Jasper broke through the pond, droplets of water cascading off his body. Their eyes locked and a ripple of emotion passed between them to match the movement of the water. It no longer mattered what they spoke out of anger. The only thing that mattered was now. In this moment. In this speck of time in the universe. Nothing else.

Charlie rose, dropping Jasper's coat that kept her warm. She undid the placket on the trousers she wore and shimmied them off her legs. The old shirt she stole from Lucas hung to her knees. She wore nothing beneath the heavy linen. There had been no need to. Charlie hated the confines of corsets and chemises. The shirt was heavy enough to hide her feminine attributes.

Jasper had not moved a muscle during her undressing. He held himself still in the pond. Charlie wished for any reaction from him. They had not broken eye contact, and he hadn't even blinked once. It was too dark for her to tell what his eyes portrayed. Did they hold desire in them? While Charlie was bold in most of her actions, her nerves screamed with an uncertainty at removing the only piece of garment covering herself. She wished Jasper would give her a sign of approval. His stillness only intensified the emotions gathering in her soul.

Jasper couldn't move a muscle, even if he wanted to. The beauty of Charlotte underneath the moonlight beam left him speechless and immobile. Her glorious mane lay in curls over her shoulders, mussed by the lateness of the night. The creamy skin she allowed him to see teased what lay beneath the shirt. The garment hit her mid-thigh, exposing silky legs that he wished Charlotte locked around his hips. Jasper's body screamed to go to Charlotte, to worship at her feet and to slide the unwanted shirt up her thighs, where he could properly worship her with his mouth. To hear her moans make music with the country sounds of darkness, while he brought them both to the brink of unrequited pleasure. Charlotte's eyes spoke of her uncertainty at his stillness. But still Jasper couldn't move.

He watched her fingers slide one button after another from its hole. The material gaped open wider, and the oversized shirt slipped off her shoulder. Jasper gulped. When she finished at the last button in the middle of her stomach, she trailed her fingers up over the exposed skin. Jasper's fingers twitched under the water at the sight. His hands closed into a fist, fighting the temptation to leave the water and take her into his embrace. The fluttering of her fingertips along the hem of the shirt displayed how unsure she was in her actions. Jasper must put a stop to this madness and act the gentleman and insist that she redress. However, Charlie's next move of boldness left Jasper speechless. All rational thoughts he might have had flew away with the light breeze.

With a recklessness Charlie never felt before, she bared herself before Jasper with a vulnerability that would make him either reject her as a gentleman or push him to act as a man driven by desire. She stood with her emotions exposed before him, offering herself. When Jasper still stood rigid, Charlie pushed past her insecurities and went to him. With each step, her confidence grew. However, before she dipped her toes into the chilly water, Jasper swung her into his arms, and his mouth descended on hers with a passion warming their very souls.

Jasper hadn't made a move toward Charlotte when she disrobed, because the picture of her naked completed the picture of a goddess tempting a mere mortal soul. He didn't know what he did to deserve her, and he didn't care. The only rational thought in his head was to make sure he didn't blunder this magnificent offering. When Charlie moved toward the water, his need to claim her prompted him out of his stupor.

His arms held her trembling body close. While Charlie brazenly stripped and attempted to join Jasper in the water, she did so full of doubts. She shook from his unspoken reaction. Now Charlie shook from anticipation. If his kisses were any sign of more to come, then Charlie would continue to tremble under Jasper's seduction.

Jasper lowered Charlotte to the ground, rising above her. "Tell me to stop."

Charlotte shook her head.

A tremor shook Jasper's body at the desire in Charlotte's eyes. No woman had ever looked at him the way she did. Every emotion Charlie held for Jasper shone forth. His hand brushed the hair from her face and cupped her cheek. The pad of his thumb stroked back and forth across her plush lips. Her tongue darted out to take a lick. When her lips pulled his finger inside her mouth, he pressed his hardness against her middle. Charlie's eyes widened at his desire, before she smiled in pleasure. If Jasper had hoped to shock Charlie into making him stop, he was sorely mistaken. Under all her unrefined attire, Charlotte Holbrooke was a temptress. Who at this very moment held Jasper under a spell. The hell with being a gentleman.

Jasper rolled over, bringing Charlie across his chest. His lips blazed a trail of fire down her neck, while his hand roamed her body, his caresses making her body arch with an ache for him to continue. When his lips found her lips again, Charlie sunk her fingers in his hair and held his head to hers. She never wanted his mouth to leave hers again. She wanted to drink from him until she couldn't breathe. And then stop only long enough to fill the air in her lungs, to continue the sweet pleasure

Charlie's grip tightened while he plundered her sweet mouth. Each kiss consumed his need to join their two bodies into one. Jasper pulled away, raising Charlie above him. Her breasts swayed before him. His head rose, taking a tempting bud between his lips. His tongue stroked the nipple while his mouth tightened, sucking harder. Charlie whimpered, her body softening in his hold. He glanced up when his mouth moved to the other tempting bud.

Charlie's gaze was fixated on his mouth near her nipple. Her eyes clouded with desire and her teeth held her bottom lip trapped in its clutches. When Jasper drew the bud in, Charlie's tongue licked out across her lips. With a groan at the erotic vision of Charlie's desire, Jasper sucked her nipple in deeply, making Charlie grow mad with the same passion.

At Charlie's husky moan, her lower body pressed against his stomach. The heat of her desire seared his chest, her wetness coating him with her need. The last of his gentlemanly honor abandoned him with that one sensation. He rolled them on the grass again, his lips searing a path to her wetness. Jasper would no longer deny himself what he craved. His sample from earlier wasn't enough. Jasper demanded everything from Charlotte. He would take from her until no other man registered a thought in her head or body.

Jasper's domination only enflamed Charlotte's need to have Jasper make her his. When his hands reached her thighs, Charlie spread her legs apart for him. Jasper didn't need to coax them open. She would do so willingly. She ached for the whisper of his kiss on her again. Only this time it wouldn't be the gentle teasing from before, but an overtaking of her senses. Charlie knew that when Jasper placed his mouth on her, the whirlwind of her emotions would fly to the highest of heights of decadence. She wasn't wrong. His mouth teased her higher and higher while his fingers stroked in and out, wringing cries of pleasures. Still, he didn't stop, but kept demanding for Charlie to give him more. Charlie sank into Jasper, giving her soul to him.

Jasper devoured Charlie. He was a thirsty man who craved this woman. He never realized how much he hungered for Charlotte. The flavor of Charlie exploded underneath him, but still he continued to appease his appetite, wanting more of her exotic sweetness. When Charlie's body tightened on the verge of a wave of pleasure, Jasper pressed his tongue against her clit, flicking rapidly until Charlie drowned him in her release. He pressed a kiss upon each thigh before he slid up her body.

Charlotte floated in a cloud of pleasure, unable to move. Her body lay heavy and relaxed into a pool of mush. Yet, Charlie still ached with a need not quite satisfied, wanting more of Jasper's loving. He took possession of her body with his mouth, now keeping the flames of her desire stroked by caressing her breasts. His touch was soft. Gentle. Sweet. Slow. His hands cupped her breasts while he placed kisses against them. Slow. Sweet. Gentle. Soft. She closed her eyes at the exquisite sensation.

Jasper placed a kiss against her lips and paused. Charlotte raised her heavy eyelids to stare into the storm blowing fiercely in Jasper's gaze.

"It will take every bit of my control I hold, but I will stop at your command, Charlotte. Tell me to stop?" Jasper's deep voice rumbled out.

Charlotte shook her head.

"Never," she whispered. "Make me yours."

Jasper growled, drawing her closer. His grip held her tightly, yet his lips drew Charlotte's in a kiss so gentle she melted. She wrapped her arms around Jasper, giving herself to him. Each of his kisses consumed her, while he pulled her leg over his hip. When his kiss deepened to enflame her desire higher, he slid inside her slowly. Charlie clung to Jasper at his body invading hers, but when his tongue stroked across hers, teasing, Charlie relaxed against him.

When Charlie trusted him with her innocence, Jasper pushed himself deep inside Charlie. Her body tensed and he held still. As soon as Charlie moaned and arched her body into his, Jasper pressed deeper, sinking himself into an abyss of paradise. His senses heightened to a higher plane of carnal pleasure. When he pulled out, Charlie moaned her displeasure and tightened around him. If this woman hadn't already brought him to his knees, her body giving him demands with her needs would have him begging for her favors. The pulsing of her core around his cock pushed him to press into her harder. When she whispered *Jasper* against his ear, he lost control.

Each stroke inside Charlotte grew longer and harder. Jasper's body demanded and took what Charlotte gave to him freely. Her hips rose and pressed with each of his strokes, demanding more from him. Charlie locked her legs around his hips, her hands clinging to his shoulders with her head thrown back. Their moans of pleasures whispered around them. Charlie's wetness pulled Jasper's cock in deeper to her throbbing core. Jasper's remaining control slipped away. He paused, watching Charlotte come undone underneath him. A sight forever etched in his memory, one he would never forget. He ground his hips against hers.

"Jasper," Charlotte cried out.

"Yes, love." He rotated his hips again.

"Love me." Charlotte stared deep into his eyes.

"With pleasure."

Jasper took Charlotte's mouth in an all-consuming kiss while their bodies exploded around them into a million sensations of pleasure. Each touch with electrifying shock wrapped them into a cocoon of passion. Their eyes locked, each of them never wanting to look away. Jasper drew Charlotte closer, both of their bodies trembling from the aftermath of their lovemaking. No words could express what they shared. Only the beating of their hearts in the silence could.

~~~~~

Charlie rode in front of Jasper. His arms wrapped lovingly around her, keeping her close. Throughout the ride he would press his lips against her head, sometimes against her cheek. Other times along her neck. Then there were the moments he brought the horse to a halt and gave her long slow kisses awakening their desires. As quickly as he would drug her with those kisses, he would end them and continue their journey back to the house.

Jasper wanted nothing more than to make love to Charlotte again, but knew they must return home before someone spotted them together. After they made love, they had laid together softy caressing one another. Whispering of their need and kissing each other into another round of frenzy. Each time they would pull back from their desire and return to the fragile forgiveness surrounding them. When the moon dipped lower their time together needed to end. He helped Charlie dress, whispering in her ears how the curve of her in the trousers tempted him with carnal thoughts.

As Charlie helped to button his shirt, her fingers stroking his chest with each button, she asked innocently of those thoughts. Which he demonstrated while he helped to button her shirt. Each stroke of his fingers against her nipples caused her breath to hitch. And when his hand lowered inside her trousers, stroking her into a fresh ache, he pulled away, declaring they must return immediately. While he only meant to tease Charlie, he ended up with a hard cock begging for release. With not enough time to take her again, he finished dressing and hurried them on their way. However, he couldn't resist kissing her along the way.

At every opportunity, the minx tempted him with pressing her backside against his cock. Then glanced over her shoulder, smiling like an innocent at him. Her hands gripped his thighs, holding onto him. Soon her hands shifted higher up his legs. Jasper grabbed her hands, bringing them in front of her, holding them tight. That wouldn't deter Charlie, though. She relaxed, showing she would stop. When Jasper relaxed his grip, Charlie brought Jasper's hands to her breasts.

Charlie laid her head back on Jasper's shoulder, sighing. She dropped her hands, and Jasper needed no more encouragement. He caressed her breasts, his thumbs brushing across her nipples. He pinched them until they tightened within his fingertips. Charlie moaned her pleasure. Her actions were wanton, and she no longer cared. Being wrapped in Jasper's arms erased every proper ladylike behavior from her mind and body. She only wanted to drive Jasper crazy with her naughty behavior. Charlotte wanted to spend the day in his arms, enjoying his pleasure and showering him with pleasure. She wanted to please Jasper with her mouth like he did her.

"Jasper?"

"Mmm."

"I want to touch you here," Charlie whispered, brushing her hand against his stiff cock.

Her touch would be his demise, but he must deny her his greatest wish. They were within sight of the house. Jasper dropped his hands from her chest and grabbed her hand from any further exploration. If anyone were to look outside, Charlie would be ruined. He had to get her inside before anyone was the wiser. Jasper planned to make right by Charlie, but on his own terms. Not by ones dictated by society, or Charlotte's uncle.

Jasper guided the horse into a spot covered in darkness, where no one would detect them. He helped Charlotte down, her body sliding against his, and she wrapped her arms around his neck. To seek his revenge from her teasing temptations on the ride back, he kissed her relentlessly, pressing her against the stable walls. When she tried to move her hands to touch him, Jasper held them suspended above her head, while he stole kiss after kiss from her lips. When her moans grew louder, Jasper stopped before he wouldn't be able to. He placed his finger against her lips before she protested.

"We must part, love, before someone catches us."

"I do not care if we are caught."

"But I do. I will not involve you in a scandal. It would ruin your good name and those of your sisters and cousin."

Charlotte knew Jasper was right, but it didn't stop her from wanting him even more. If anything the danger of getting caught held the same edge that always provoked Charlie into trouble. Only this time there was much more at stake. Even though neither one of them spoke of love, Charlie's heart felt Jasper would take care of her. The passion they shared could only be love. It was too strong to be anything less.

"Will you walk me around back to the servant's entrance?" asked Charlie.

Jasper nodded, lacing his fingers through hers and bringing them to his lips for a kiss. With his other hand, he looped the reins around the fence. He would return later to take care of the horse. For now he would see Charlie safe inside and to her bedroom. He wouldn't leave her alone to explain her whereabouts in case she ran into someone. It wouldn't be fair.

They slipped inside the back door and made their way up the staircase. When they reached the landing, Jasper pressed a soft kiss against Charlie's lips. Before the kiss could go any further, he gently pushed her toward her bedroom door. Charlotte turned at the door and smiled shyly before she slipped inside. Jasper breathed a sigh of relief at her safe arrival. He crept down the stairs, eager to leave the family wing of the estate before he ran into any member of Charlotte's family. He didn't want to explain his presence.

Little did Sinclair know that someone had already witnessed his exchange with Charlotte. The very person who had watched Charlotte sneak off into the darkness occupied the chair at the end of the hallway. An alarm wouldn't be called on what was obviously Charlotte's ruination. However, the gentleman would now have to fight for the lady's hand in a healthy competition. If he won, Sinclair would have to prove his true intentions toward the lady by sacrificing his prize if the lady didn't believe in his love.

Chapter Thirteen

"Charlie, wake up." Evelyn shook Charlotte's shoulder.

Charlie snuggled deeper under the covers, ignoring her sister's plea. The remnant of a dream hovered on the brink of disappearing forever. She didn't want to lose the lingering memories. They were too delicious to part with. Jasper had been making love to her with his mouth. The memory sent a tingle throughout Charlie's body. Perhaps she should awaken, find Jasper, and they could continue where they left off the night before. A smile spread across Charlie's face. Her body grew warm in anticipation for Jasper's touch.

"Charlie, you must wake up now." Evelyn persisted.

"Mmm, why the urgency, Evie?" Charlie teased Evelyn with the nickname her sister hated.

"Why do I bother to help you when you insist on pushing the boundaries of acceptable behavior?"

Charlotte stretched, feeling the tenderness between her thighs when she moved. Which only brought forth another smile. She would endure a million more of those aches to have Jasper make love to her again.

"You bother, because you love me." Charlie opened her eyes to find Evelyn standing over her, agitated, glancing over her shoulder at the door.

Evelyn waved her hand in annoyance and rushed to the door, looking along the hallway. She closed the door quietly, came back to the bed, and yanked the covers away from Charlie. Evelyn tugged Charlie off the bed, shoving a dress in her arms. She motioned for Charlie to get behind the dressing screen.

"Hurry," Evelyn ordered.

Charlie frowned at Evelyn's odd behavior, but followed her command. Charlie stepped behind the screen and pulled off her nightgown. Lying on the bench were a chemise and stockings. With Evelyn's rush to see Charlie dressed, she wouldn't have time for a corset. Which was fine with Charlie, because she detested the things. Charlie slipped on her clothing. She would have loved a bath to soothe her aching body, or at least a washcloth to freshen herself. However, Charlie knew her sister wouldn't allow those luxuries with her demanding nature this morning.

"What is the hurry, Evelyn?" Charlie asked.

Charlotte's head was bent, coming out from behind the screen, tying the ribbon in the front of her dress. When she raised her head, Charlie watched Evelyn playing servant and making Charlie's bed. Once Evelyn put the bed to rights, she bustled behind Charlotte and played lady's maid, buttoning her dress. Then Evelyn shoved Charlie in a chair and yanked the brush through Charlie's hair. The entire time Evelyn kept muttering to herself, but not loud enough for Charlie to understand her rantings. Evelyn tied a ribbon in Charlie's hair, then dragged Charlie to the chaise against the window, forcing her down. Evelyn opened a book and placed it in Charlie's hand. Her sister went to open the door, returning to sit in the chair next to the chaise. Evelyn picked up her sewing and pointed to the book.

"Read aloud."

Charlotte sat confused from the whirlwind activity. She had barely woken from her stimulating dream before Evelyn forced her to get ready for the day. Not to mention, Charlie was starving. Her stomach rumbled its discomfort. Evelyn's behavior was most confusing. Charlie would play along for now, but she really wanted to eat. She hoped Cook sent up some berry pastries with the hot chocolate. Charlie desired something sweet for breakfast.

A pounding of loud footsteps started coming down the hallway. She listened to Jacqueline urging Aunt Susanna not to bother Charlie. The voices of Gemma and Abigail agreed with Jacqueline. Charlie also heard Selina Pemberton's snide remarks, degrading Charlie's character. Finally, Aunt Susanna stopped right before the door and announced for the ladies to be silent.

"Evelyn, what is the fuss this morning?" Charlie whispered.

"Oh, Charlotte. 'Tis not morning, but two in the afternoon. Just follow my lead. Now read aloud to me."

Charlotte now understood the full impact of Evelyn's odd behavior. She had never slept so late before. Was there more to this, though? Had somebody seen Jasper and her passionate exchange last night? The tone of Evelyn's voice spoke her disappointment. Charlie's selfish actions put Evelyn's happiness in jeopardy. Charlie reached out to grab Evelyn's hand. She squeezed it and mouthed *I am sorry*. Evelyn nodded in understanding, squeezing her hand to show her forgiveness.

The repercussions of Charlie's actions slammed in her gut. She started reading, her voice barely above a whisper. With the lateness of her lie-in, no corset, and the stage Evelyn set of Charlie laying on the chaise, reading a book, Evelyn must have pleaded sickness for Charlie's absence from today's activities. Charlie wouldn't prove Evelyn false, she would keep up the pretense long enough to appease Jacqueline and Aunt Susanna. However, Charlie knew they didn't fool Jacqueline. Her older sister realized something was afoot, and once they pacified Aunt Susanna, Jacqueline would demand the truth.

"Ladies, please return to the parlor. I do not wish for any of you to catch Charlotte's illness. I will appraise you of her recovery shortly," said Aunt Susanna.

The footsteps retreated down the hallway before Aunt Susanna swept into the room, making her way to Charlotte's side. She rested on the seat in front of Charlie, placing a hand on Charlie's forehead.

"Mmm, you are not warm. Are you ill?" Aunt Susanna asked.

"No, Aunty. I am over-tired from the daily activities and the full evening entertainments. I am sorry for causing worry, I only wished to rest for the day."

"Pshh." Jacqueline muttered, glaring at Charlie. Her older sister always saw through her lies.

Aunt Susanna patted Charlie's hand in understanding. "Yes, yes. I understand, dear. This week has been out of the norm for you girls. You especially, Charlotte, with the way Lord Sinclair and Lord Worthington have favored their attentions your way. Why, who would have guessed that not one but two of London's most eligible bachelors would have pursued you? Not that you are not worthy of such treatment. I understand how you view the entire business of courtship. So, have you made a choice, my dear? It would not be proper to lead the gentlemen on, if you were not interested. No matter how tempting of an offer your uncle dangled for them to win your heart."

"What has Uncle Theo done?"

"Nothing, nothing. Just the ramblings of an old lady who is throwing a successful house party. Now, shall we expect you at dinner? Or do you need to rest longer?"

"I am well rested for dinner."

"Fabulous. Now, who shall I sit you by? Worthington or Sinclair?"

Sinclair was on the tip of Charlie's tongue, but Evelyn mouthed for Charlie to answer Worthington. Since Evelyn had covered for her, it was the least she could do. Not that she wouldn't get to sit by Jasper. She must convince Aunt Susanna to place Evelyn next to Jasper.

"Lord Worthington."

"Strange, I thought you would have said Lord Sinclair. But the heart knows what the heart wants. What is even more strange now that I think about it, Lord Sinclair must have had a late night too, since he did not rise until noon. Am I overdoing the entertainments?"

They reassured Aunt Susanna that she'd paced the activities out evenly. Her sisters however turned questioning looks upon Charlie. She saw them come to the same conclusion. Would the guests also make the connection? If Selina did, the rumor mill would begin. Selina would take great pleasure on proving Charlie and Jasper were in a scandalous relationship.

"Perhaps you could sit Evelyn next to Lord Sinclair?" Charlie suggested.

"No, I cannot do that. It will only confuse the gentleman if he has feelings for you. That would not be fair to Evelyn. I shall sit Evelyn between Lord Ralston and Lord Kincaid for this evening. Will that be acceptable, Evelyn?"

"Yes," answered Evelyn.

Charlotte inwardly sighed. Of course, it would be all right for Evelyn. The man who Evelyn most desired would be *her* dinner partner. Charlie's evening was destined for boredom. Neither of the gentlemen was one she wished to keep company. Lord Kincaid was one of Lucas's best mates. Too serious, never finding Charlie's hijinks amusing. Kincaid always tried to discipline her. Then there was Lord Ralston, a more unscrupulous, womanizing, arrogant rake if there ever was one. He had only secured an invitation to the house party because Lord Ralston's father was Uncle Theo's friend. There were rumors Uncle Theo held Lord Ralston's markers. It was a well-known fact that Lord Ralston gambled and lost quite heavily. So Charlie would have to endure dinner caught between a stick in the mud and a scoundrel, when she only wanted to sit next to Jasper. What one would sacrifice for their sister's happiness.

"Now I shall order a bath for you to relax in. Pamper yourself for the afternoon, so you are fresh for dinner. Please stay away from the stables. If you want to draw Lord Worthington's attention, smelling like horses is not the way to entice a man to fall in love. Even if his love of horses matches yours."

As quickly as Aunt Susanna had bustled in, she left in the same manner. Which left Charlie alone with Evelyn and Jaqueline. Her sisters would want answers. Answers Charlie wasn't ready to confess. She wanted to keep the secret of Jasper to herself for a while longer. At least until she knew his intentions. After they'd made love, they hadn't discussed the future. Jasper made her no promises. Before her sisters questioned Charlie, Gemma and Abigail slipped in the room, closing the door behind them. They crawled on Charlie's bed, waiting. All of them waited for Charlie to explain her absence. It would appear that she wouldn't get to keep her secrets to herself after all.

"Please tell me there is no relation to Sinclair's lateness of rising and yours," said Jacqueline.

Even if Charlie were to deny Jacqueline's accusation, the blush spreading across her cheeks would speak the truth. Charlie lowered her head, pretending interest in the book. Her fingers ran back and forth across the edges of the spine. She felt their eyes on her. If she raised her head, she would encounter looks of amusement, disappointment, sympathy, excitement, and most of all acceptance. That was why she loved her family so much. They might call her foolish or reprimand her, but none of them would hold a low opinion or judge her actions.

"Oh Charlie, how romantic," Gemma sighed.

"But no great surprise," murmured Abigail.

"What do you mean, no great surprise?" asked Charlie.

"It has been more than obvious this last year," answered Abigail.

"Obvious how?"

Abigail glanced around the bedroom. "Am I the only one who has noticed?"

Everyone but Charlie answered no.

"Noticed what?" Charlie held no clue what the others had seen that she hadn't.

Jacqueline sighed, sitting on Evelyn's bed. "The attraction building between Sinclair and you."

"What nonsense. There has been no sign of attraction until the day we played pall-mall and he first kissed me."

"Do you mean the day that you and Evelyn first switched identities?" Jacqueline asked.

"You knew?" Evelyn and Charlie asked at the same time.

Jacqueline shook her head at them. "Did you two believe that you have fooled anyone with your game?"

"Yes," they answered.

Gemma and Abigail shook their heads too.

"Well, maybe not you three, but we have fooled everyone else," said Charlie.

"Perhaps the other guests. Maybe even Lucas. I am sure your Uncle Theo has figured it out," said Abigail.

"Aunt Susanna?" asked Evelyn.

"Oh yes, definitely, Aunt Susanna has," laughed Gemma.

"Then why did she ..." started Charlie.

"Ask who you wished to sit by? Why, to convince you she is ignorant of your switch. She sides with Uncle Theo on this matchmaking attempt. Aunt Susanna would like each of us to settle with a gentleman from this party. She does not wish to play chaperone in London, but if she has to, she does not want to debut five ladies at once," explained Jacqueline.

"Four," said Abigail.

"Five," answered Gemma firmly.

"That still does not answer my questions."

"Which question was that?" asked Jacqueline.

"All of them," answered Charlie.

"Will you answer *my* question?" asked Jacqueline.

Charlie nodded. For her to understand what they had told her, she would need to be honest with them. No matter what the consequences held.

"Where you alone with Jasper Sinclair last night?"

"Yes."

"Did he take advantage of you?"

"No."

"When does he plan to make an offer for you?"

"That did not come up for discussion."

"He does plan to?" asked Abigail.

Charlie shrugged, she held no clue on Jasper's intentions. While her heart knew he would, she couldn't speak for him.

"Oh, Charlotte," said Jacqueline.

"He will, Jasper Sinclair is an honest gentleman. He would not have ruined Charlie with no plans to do right by her." Evelyn came to Sinclair's defense.

Charlie smiled at her sister's declaration of faith. She didn't doubt Jasper either. It felt nice that her sister believed in him too.

"Can you explain how all of you knew about the attraction between Jasper and I, when I did not?"

"When no one is looking, Jasper's eyes follow you around the room. His attention never strays from you. His eyes devour you," Gemma sighed. Always the romantic.

"Do not forget his jealousy when other men take interest in Charlie. Whenever Charlie talks to another man, he joins the conversation," said Abigail.

"That is only because we share similar interests," objected Charlie.

"If you were not around, he would inquire to your health or your whereabouts. Once he was told, he would seek you out," Evelyn piped in.

"To be candid, the air crackles with the attraction between you two," said Jacqueline.

Charlie sat silently, listening to her family's opinion. When she thought about the last few months, their comments rang true. There had been a shift in their relationship. They were so minor that Charlie hadn't noticed. Since Jasper had been a constant in her life for as long as she could remember, she didn't realize her feelings for him had grown stronger.

"If you say Aunt Susanna knows that Evelyn and I are switching identities, then she must know that we will tonight and it will be Evelyn sitting next to Worthington. Why does she refuse to sit me next to Jasper at dinner?"

"Because she enjoys the drama of watching Jasper Sinclair unhinge over you. Sinclair is a confident gentleman who is always a charmer. However, since this party started, his behavior is erratic where you are concerned. I believe she wishes to keep the party lively with Sinclair and you as entertainment. You should have seen the glee that lit her face at your greeting toward Duncan yesterday and Sinclair's jealous reaction. No, she will not sit you next to him. She will take pleasure when Sinclair stews over the attention Kincaid and Ralston will pay you," said Jacqueline.

"Kincaid will not pay attention to me and I do not think I am Ralston's type. There will be nothing to see."

"Lord Ralston will flirt with anything within his eyesight. Well, that is everyone except me," muttered Gemma.

Charlie had been about to ask Gemma if she wished for Lord Ralston to flirt with her, but decided now was not the time. She would not embarrass Gemma or cause her discomfort, just because she wanted to distract them from her follies. When Charlie found some time to be alone with Gemma, she would ask her cousin if she harbored feelings for the rake. If she did, then she would help Gemma, the same as she helped Evelyn. Charlie now understood that she had fallen in love with Jasper long before this house party had begun. Now she wanted her entire family to find the same love.

"Charlotte, men are strange creatures. Even more so after they have been intimate with a woman. Believe me, Sinclair will become very possessive of you from here on out. And watching Ralston flirt with you while he cannot intervene will be a sight," explained Jacqueline.

"What should I do?"

"You should flirt with Ralston. Force Sinclair to ask for your hand, before Lucas discovers the truth. Selina is determined to ruin you. If she catches even a whiff of any scandal surrounding you, she will smear your name amongst the ton," said Abigail.

"No, I will not force Jasper's hand. I do not want anyone to pressure him, when I know in my heart he will ask me on his own terms. I am not afraid of Selina and her schemes."

Everyone, including Charlie, knew that she should be. Selina had been on the warpath towards Charlie ever since the party started. It didn't help the prank she'd pulled on Selina when she arrived. Charlie didn't tell the other girls about what she had done, since Selina never made a scene about it. But Charlie realized that Selina discovered that it was her who had replaced her hairbrush with a horse brush from the stable. It may have been petty, but Charlie wanted to seek revenge against Selina after she was so cruel to Abigail at their morning ritual. While their manners were impolite in not inviting her, they remedied that the following day by inviting all the female guests to join them for hot chocolate. However, Selina never came, and instead she mocked the other guests, alienating herself more. Charlie held no sympathy for Selina.

"Now that we understand your newfound romance with Sinclair, shall we discuss the matter of Evelyn and Worthington? Please explain why the two of you needed to switch identities where that gentleman is concerned," asked Jacqueline.

Charlie shared a look with Evelyn, encouraging her to confide her secret. When this first began, they foolishly believed they could handle the deception. However, the longer it continued, their plan created more trouble. They were in over their heads and nowhere nearer to having Worthington fall in love with Evelyn. There were only a couple of days left before the ball. After that, Worthington would head to London to find a bride before returning home to his estate. Evelyn would arrive too late to pursue him during the season. No, it must be this week. If not, Uncle Theo would marry her off to another gentleman, one that Evelyn didn't love.

"Over the Christmas holidays when Worthington was a guest, we shared a few kisses in the library."

"Oh Evelyn," Jacqueline sighed.

"Only Worthington thought he had kissed Charlie," continued Evelyn.

All eyes swiveled to Jacqueline, waiting for her to voice her disappointment and for her to reprimand them. When she rose from the chaise and paced across the rug, four sets of eyes tracked her. Waiting. The air in the room grew thick with dread. Evelyn and Charlotte looked to Jacqueline for guidance in life and never wanted for Jacqueline to be ashamed of them.

"While I do not approve of your actions, I cannot scold you for them either. Your behavior reminds me of when we were young, before mama and papa died. The two of you would constantly cause mischief when you pretended to be each other. Papa would have to rescue you from your scrapes. Mama would scold you, then her laughter would ring through the house of the amusement you caused. This past week has reminded me of those times, and that is why I have not put a halt to your antics. Even when Sinclair urged me to do so, I refused. After our parents death, I have had to watch the two of you close yourselves off into your shells. When they died, part of us died too. All of us lost a part of ourselves that dreadful day. Evelyn, you retreated from life, too afraid to live, to allow yourself to grow close to another. While Charlie, you acted out with one ridiculous escapade after another. Each time you pushed your limits closer and closer to danger."

Jacqueline paused and continued her pacing. It was as if she was trying to form her thoughts into the right words.

"But this week I have watched both of you blossom into the amazing ladies I believed you could be. Evelyn, you emerged from your shell and came alive. Your laughter and participation throughout the house party has been a balm to my soul. It has been a pleasure to watch you. Even you, Charlie, while you might still act before thinking, I see you do it out of love and not to harm yourself."

Tears slid along Charlie's cheeks. The love she felt for her sisters overwhelmed her. She hadn't realized the anguish she had caused her sister through the years. After listening to Jacqueline, Charlie now realized her rebellion had been an act to cope with her parent's deaths. Charlie had never healed from losing them. Even now with her falling in love with Jasper, she wished her parents were alive to share her joy. While they wouldn't be so understanding of her actions, they would support her.

Charlie uncurled from the chaise at the same time that Evelyn rose from the chair. They both ran to Jacqueline and hugged her. Their emotions were raw from Jacqueline's speech. They all started blubbering their love, then laughed at themselves. When they heard Abigail and Gemma crying on the bed, they opened their arms for them. The two girls joined them as they had done many times through the years.

A knock on the door drew them apart. Polly bustled in, followed by servants carrying buckets of water for Charlie's bath. They filled the tub and Polly opened Charlie's wardrobe, pulling out the garments Charlie would need for dinner. Another maid walked in carrying a tea tray and a platter of sandwiches. Also on the tray rested a plate of mouthwatering pastries.

"Lady Forrester said to pamper you for the afternoon, miss. She ordered for you to take a bath and eat. Then you are to rest before dinner."

"Thank you, Polly. We will help Charlie with her bath and make sure she rests. You can return to dress Charlotte and Evelyn for dinner," Jacqueline ordered Polly.

"Yes, my lady."

"Polly?"

Polly turned. "Yes?"

"Please dress Evelyn and Charlotte's hair in the exact same ribbons." Jacqueline winked.

A conspiring smile swept across Polly's face before she nodded and left.

"Now Charlie, into the bath. Ladies, shall we enjoy this repast while we concoct a plan to bring Lord Worthington to Evelyn's knees?" asked Jacqueline.

Chapter Fourteen

Sinclair descended the stairs at a leisurely pace, not wanting to attract attention toward himself. He had risen later than his usual early morning hour. Thoughts of Charlotte had kept him awake when he had finally found his bed. A secret smile slipped as he remembered the temptress. Without making it too obvious, he hoped to locate Charlotte and persuade her to sneak away with him. When he walked into the dining room, he searched for her but came up empty. The table was full of animated conversations between the other guests. Sinclair walked to the buffet against the wall and told the footman what he wanted. He slipped into a seat unnoticed and ate his lunch, listening to the conversation floating around him. When he overheard Evelyn make the excuse of Charlie feeling ill, he wanted to rush to her side and take care of her. Lady Forrester and Jacqueline said they would visit her after lunch. After their comment, Evelyn appeared nervous. Was Charlie sick or had she snuck out undetected? Soon Evelyn excused herself, rushing from the room. Sinclair wished to follow, but knew he wouldn't be able to see Charlie alone. His stare at the entry way caused Lady Selina Pemberton to comment.

"Lord Sinclair, did you enjoy the gentlemen's evening a little too much or were you involved in other activities that kept you in your bed throughout the morning? I hope you did not catch whatever inflection Lady Charlotte is suffering from."

"Selina," her father warned.

"I am wondering over a guest's welfare, Father. Before long I will be mistress over this household and it would be inconsiderate of me not to show my concern. I am sorry, Your Grace and Lord Sinclair, if I have overstepped my bounds." Lady Selina offered a meek smile to the Duke of Colebourne.

The fluttering of eyelashes and innocent smile didn't fool Sinclair for one minute. Selina had tried catching Charlie and him yesterday, and today she was trying to cause speculation toward them.

"Thank you for your concern, Lady Selina. I am afraid I imbibed in too many spirits last night. A mistake I will not make again for a while. Whiskey is a devil's drink if not consumed at a leisurely pace."

The other gentlemen around the table laughed in agreement. Before Selina could draw Charlotte back into the conversation, the married husbands received reprimands for their overindulgence from the night before. Lady Forrester changed the subject from the unsavory conversation around the innocent ladies.

Sinclair nodded at Selina. She narrowed her eyes, not believing him. While he stopped her from voicing her speculations for now, he knew it wouldn't be for long. Lady Selina wanted Charlie involved in a scandal. He wondered what the minx had done to provoke the attack. Sinclair would need to convince Charlie to stop her ploys against Selina. Charlie had to accept the fact that Gray would marry the chit and there was nothing she could do to prevent it.

Jasper finished his meal, interjecting comments in here and there to the conversations. After an acceptable amount of time, he rose from the table. He meant to find Charlotte and see about her illness. He grew concerned that their love-making had been too much for her. She would be tender, and he was a bastard for taking her the way he did on the ground. Charlotte had deserved better.

"Sinclair?"

Sinclair turned when the Duke of Colebourne spoke. The duke sat relaxed at the table.

"Yes?"

"Please join me in my study in a half-hour's time." The duke didn't ask, nor was it a demand. Only a simple request of what the duke expected of Sinclair.

Sinclair nodded before taking his leave. Now he couldn't seek out Charlotte. Instead, he felt like her uncle would demand a marriage between them. This wasn't what he wanted for them. He wanted to woo her and propose to her during the ball. Sinclair planned to return to his estate tomorrow, where he would inform his mother of his plans and ask for his grandmother's ring to give to Charlie. His mother would be ecstatic. She had been pressuring Jasper to find a bride. Even mentioning Charlotte's name many times. And every time Sinclair had scoffed, unaware of how the chit affected him. And every time his mother would smile, then change the subject. It was always enough though to make him question. Now Sinclair knew the answer. The exact moment he fell in love with Charlotte Holbrooke, he couldn't recall. Only now he understood that he couldn't remember not loving her.

Not waiting to reach the half hour, Sinclair walked to the duke's study. However, once he entered the room, he saw he wasn't the only gentleman present. Gray and Forrester relaxed on the sofa, talking about Duncan's estate. Forrester glared at Sinclair, but Gray only nodded in greeting. If the duke called him to the study to discuss his involvement in Charlotte's ruination, then Gray wouldn't have been so polite. He would have torn

Sinclair limb from limb defending his cousin's honor. Still unsure of the reason for the duke's demand, he chose a chair as far from the members of Charlotte's family that he could sit.

He glanced at the clock to see that the time for the meeting drew near. Sinclair watched each hand tick to the next minute. His thoughts scrambled together an apology and an explanation for his behavior. All the times his father called him into the study for discipline never prepared him for this. It was agony waiting for the duke to call him out. However, when the other eligible bachelors started arriving and taking a seat, Sinclair grew confused. If the duke didn't call him here to discuss his inappropriate behavior toward his niece, then what did this meeting concern?

The duke stepped into his study, regarding the gentlemen awaiting his request. The meeting was only meant for one gentleman, but he'd invited the others to determine if the one gentleman would state his intentions toward his niece. When Sinclair never came to him that morning but lazed in bed, Colebourne decided to make the man suffer for ruining his niece. He thought highly of Sinclair and assumed the gentleman would make an offer for Charlotte. Instead, Sinclair came into luncheon and never requested a meeting, acting nonchalant. This angered Colebourne. Perhaps the gentleman wasn't the man for Charlotte. He'd noticed Worthington paying Charlotte attention. Maybe he was the gentleman for her? However, Colebourne knew what Worthington had not figured out. Worthington thought he was courting Charlotte when all along it was Evelyn. His nieces had weaved a fine web he needed to untangle before this house party ended. A simple enticement would bring Sinclair to scratch.

Colebourne slipped behind his desk, leaning back in his chair. He lit a cigar, peering out behind the smoke, giving each gentleman a formable glare. He chuckled to himself when he noted a few of the men squirm in their chairs. Especially Sinclair. Today he would focus on making Sinclair uncomfortable, the other gentleman he would leave for a later date.

"It has come to my attention that a certain lady has been taken advantage of during this house party by one of you. Since none of you have stepped forward to ask for the lady, I have an enticement to offer you," said the Duke of Colebourne.

"Who has been ruined?" Gray stood in a fit of anger.

"Charlotte." The duke let the lady's name dangle in the air.

Sinclair shot a glare at Forrester, who lifted his shoulder in a shrug of denial. Then he looked over to Worthington, who appeared nervous. Sinclair's eyes narrowed. What did Worthington have to be uncomfortable about? Had he compromised Charlotte? No, wait, the girls always switched places. Worthington would have dallied with Evelyn thinking it was Charlotte. What a mess.

"Who ruined her?" Gray snarled.

It was apparent Gray hadn't been paying attention to his cousins throughout the house party. Could it be because Lady Selina was in attendance, or because his thoughts were more centered on Abigail? Gray's feelings regarding the young miss didn't go unnoticed by Sinclair. When Gray thought no one looked, his stare fixated on the beauty. However, Gray couldn't ever act because of his betrothal.

"I have decided not to name the gentleman. Instead I will make the offer of Sapphire's foal to the gentleman who charms my niece to the marriage altar. Since the fool did not ask for an appointment to offer for Charlotte's hand, then perhaps he does not deserve her."

Kincaid stood, pulling the sleeves of his coat down. "Since I have no interest in the chit or the horse, I will decline your offer. You can trust me to stay silent on this matter. I have no wish to tarnish the girl's reputation, just because she laid her trust with one of these scoundrels." Kincaid left the study.

"I am not guilty either, but I will accept this tempting offer. I would not mind the chit. She is easy on one's eyes. And feisty, too. No offense, Your Grace," said Ralston.

"None taken, Ralston."

"Perhaps Lady Forrester would be so inclined to sit me next to Lady Charlotte at dinner this evening."

"I think that can be arranged." A devious smile lit the duke's face when he answered Ralston, while staring at Sinclair.

The only emotion and sign of anger Sinclair showed was how his hands gripped the chair's arm rest. His fingers dug into the carved wood. Sinclair's teeth gritted, trying to hold back the denial he wanted to rage. The duke wished to provoke him into declaring himself the man who ruined Charlotte, but he stayed silent. The duke could dangle his offer all he wanted, but in the end Charlie would choose him. That, he held faith in. No man would force him until he was ready to declare his intentions. Not even the Duke of Colebourne.

"Excellent. I shall see you gentlemen at dinner." Ralston strutted out the door.

Forrester broke the heavy silence with a chuckle. "What a quandary you have, Uncle Theo. I do not envy the man when you expose your true wrath."

"Funny you should mention my wrath, my boy." The duke quirked an eyebrow at his nephew.

"What? I have not ruined Charlie."

"Mmm, one would say your midnight rendezvous with the girl was not completely innocent. Then there is the matter of another girl in attendance you dallied with. One I have every right to call you out on, but she is not my ward, so I cannot. I can only issue you a warning. Stay clear, she is not yours."

"Well, in that case, consider me in." Forrester stood and bowed to his uncle.

"Like hell," Sinclair snarled.

"Well, Sinclair has stated his opinion, what do you say, Worthington?"

"It would be an honor to win Lady Charlotte's hand."

The pompous ass stood and shook the duke's hand. Sinclair watched in disgust. This was why one did not lie in bed for a half a day. It sent the rest of the day into hell. Sinclair had lost his chance to ever get Charlotte alone, because half the men in attendance would now seek her attention.

"May the best man win." The duke swung his feet on the desk, inhaling a long drag of the cigar. His stare stating his feelings toward Sinclair.

Sinclair stomped from the room all the way outdoors. His steps led to the stable, and the rest of the men watched him push his horse into a run. The horse kicked up the loose dirt, leaving a storm in its wake. Worthington exited in a much quieter manner. The duke motioned for Forrester to take his leave too. Once the duke remained in the room with his son, he let out the sigh of a weary uncle worried over his ward.

"When this house party is over, I will sign your admittance into Bedlam," said Lucas.

"There will be no need, my boy."

"So which of them do I need to call out?"

"I will take care of the gentleman, if he does not come up to snuff."

"Why not call him out now?"

"Because if I force him, then Charlie will always wonder if the bloke truly loved her or if he married her by force."

Lucas sighed. "I understand your point. But if any of our guests learn of the scandal, you cannot take any of them to London for a season and will have to offer bribes for them to marry."

"I am aware of the consequences. However, the gentleman will propose within the next two days. Of that I am sure."

Lucas trusted his father to make the right decision for Charlotte and the other girls. However, there was only one girl on his mind and it wasn't his fiancée. He wondered if his father knew of Abigail's plans.

"I overhead Abigail talking to Aunt Susanna yesterday."

"Yes, they converse quite frequently. They even correspond when your aunt returns home."

"Do you know Abigail plans to leave home after all the girls marry? She wants to become a paid companion or governess."

"Yes, Susanna informed me of Abigail's plans."

"She cannot do that. No member of our family will work for money."

"We have no control over Abigail. She is free to do what she wishes. I only had guardianship over her until she reached the age of twenty-one. When she came of age, I informed her of the trust I set up in her name. However, she refuses to touch the money."

"We must convince her to stay. Did you speak of your plans for her to have a London season too?"

"Yes, I even informed her of the dowry I have secured for her."

"I do not understand her need to leave then."

"Do you not?"

"No." Lucas looked at his father in confusion.

"Then perhaps it is for the best that she leaves."

"You do not believe that."

His father didn't answer him. Lucas couldn't understand what his father was getting at. Before this house party started, his father was adamant that Abigail join the other girls for a London season. All these years, Abigail had been a member of their family and his father protected her just as fiercely as he did his cousins. Why would his father allow Abigail to leave? Ever since this house party started, life had been off-balance.

"I will concern myself with Abigail. You need to focus your interest on Lady Selina. Her father has complained to me of your neglect. It is time that we move this betrothal forward. At the end of the house party, I will discuss the settlements with Selina's father. Then we will set a date for the wedding."

"If you insist."

"I insist."

Colebourne watched his only child, lost in thought. The poor boy hadn't even realized yet that he loved the girl. It was more than obvious to all. Well, to everyone but the boy and the girl. Abigail herself was as much in love with Lucas as he was her. They were both too blind to see it. But in time, he had a plan to bring the two together. Oh, he was a fool all those years ago to tie Lucas to Selina Pemberton. He realized the error of his ways. Colebourne only hoped it wasn't too late. With a little nudge, his womanizing nephew would take the matters out of his hands. A certain kiss between the two confirmed Colebourne's suspicion. A devious smile lit his face once again. Playing matchmaker gave him a new zest for life. It wouldn't be long before he bounced his grandchildren and great niece and nephews on his knees.

Chapter Fifteen

Sinclair leaned against the fireplace mantel, nursing his drink. He didn't want the whiskey, but Gray had been insistent on joining him. Gray ranted about the offer his father made for Charlotte. He wanted to know if Sinclair had a clue on who ruined Charlie. Gray continued to tell Sinclair how he would rip the bastard apart with his two hands once he found out. Sinclair cringed at the fury contained in his friend. He felt guilty for keeping the truth from Gray, and his need to avoid bodily harm kept him quiet. Should he feel offended that Gray didn't accuse him? Did Gray consider Sinclair not good enough for Charlie? Was Gray that clueless not to figure out that Sinclair was the guilty party by his outburst earlier? Or was this a test for Sinclair to confess? Either way, the truth would come out soon. Hopefully, after he surprised Charlie with his proposal.

When Sinclair had stormed away, he rode like the devil to his estate. He surprised his mother when he demanded his grandmother's ring. Her surprise didn't last long, before she became excited that he had finally chosen a bride. Sinclair followed his mother to her bedroom, while she searched for the ring. She kept talking about weddings, the church, and when a perfect time would be for the ceremony. Then she started talking about babies. How she longed to be a grandmother.

Sinclair stood there calling himself all sorts of a fool. In his state of desire, he thought of nothing but making Charlie his. He failed to protect her. Charlotte might carry his baby now. He sat on the edge of his mother's bed while she rambled on, the impact of his actions hitting him. In that moment, every emotion he held for Charlotte consumed him. But it was the love he realized he held for her forever that settled him. He smiled at his mother's fantasies about babies. Sinclair couldn't wait to see Charlie grow with their child. She would be a wonderful and caring mother. Little wonders who would have their mother's sense of adventure.

Then his mother handed him the ring, squeezing his hand around it and asked, "Is it Charlie?" Sinclair heard the hope in his mother's voice. His mother loved Charlie as much as he did. His mother accepted Charlie for Charlie. Not as Charlotte, but as Charlie. Sinclair wanted to answer yes, but didn't. Charlie would be the first to learn of his intentions before anyone else.

"It is a secret for now. I want the lady I have chosen to be the first to know. But understand that I love her with all my heart and you will too."

His mother kissed his cheek. "If you love her, then I will too."

Sinclair left, with all intentions to return to the house party. However, his stable master cornered him with a problem. A repair they were making to the stables needed an extra hand to finish. Sinclair labored the rest of the afternoon trying to raise a new wall on the stables. By the time he had returned, he only had enough time to bathe and change his clothes for dinner. Sinclair ran out of time to steal a few precious moments with Charlie. Hopefully, after dinner he would have a chance.

Now he waited for her to join the rest of the party in the drawing room. Charlie and Evelyn were the last to arrive. Everyone was waiting for them before they proceeded to the dining room. His need to see Charlie kept him focused on the entryway. When she finally appeared, his heart stopped. Evelyn and Charlie appeared at the same time with their arms locked together. However, Charlotte was the only lady who captured Sinclair's attention.

She looked lovely with ribbons holding her hair in a flattering design. Charlie wore a lovely pale blue creation, with a pink chiffon ribbon tied around her middle. A shy smile lit her face and her eyes flittered around the room until they landed on him. Her smile grew wider. Jasper's heart started again at her smile. He reached up to pat his pocket over his heart to make sure the ring was secure, not realizing the gesture until after he did it. But the pink blush spreading across Charlotte's cheek was worth it. Jasper took a step, wanting to go to her.

Gray's hand grabbed his shoulder. "We shall see which bastard goes to her, then we will know who ruined her."

Before Sinclair could shake Gray's hold, Worthington approached the two ladies. Only he couldn't tell them apart. Sinclair looked more closely and saw the similarities. Both of them had their hair styled the same, even down to the exact color of ribbon. While Charlie's dress was a pale blue, Evelyn wore a similar creation in a pale green. Evelyn's ribbon around her waist matched Charlotte's. Both of them wore matching pearl necklaces and ear bobs. Which would only be in Sinclair's favor.

"I thought it was him. And to think I called him my friend," Gray muttered.

Sinclair let Gray believe Worthington was the gentleman who ruined Charlie. It took the pressure off him. Gray wouldn't watch over Sinclair's actions, because he would be distracted by following Worthington. Also, with the sisters switching identities, which they planned on doing again this evening by dressing the same, Gray would follow Evelyn and Worthington. So, Sinclair should be able to sneak away with Charlie.

"Now that the twins have arrived, we shall proceed to dinner," announced Lady Forrester. Then she started directing the gentlemen on which lady to escort. When Worthington was told to escort Charlotte he stood confused on which lady to offer his arm. Sinclair watched Charlie step back and gently push Evelyn toward Worthington. Jasper smiled that he was correct on what would play out this evening. He hoped Lady Forrester would suggest for him to take Evelyn's arm, but she choose Lord Ralston for that privilege.

Sinclair wanted to growl at this. When he caught the Duke of Colebourne's gaze, the duke raised his glass as a signal that he knew everything that went on in his home. The duke knew the twins had switched places, and even though Ralston was clueless, the duke honored Ralston's request of sitting next to Charlie during dinner. What Sinclair did next would gain the duke's respect for years to come. Sinclair raised his glass, accepting the challenge. Not even the duke would keep him from what his heart most desired. Charlotte.

Sinclair escorted Jacqueline into dinner. After he helped her into a seat, he sat in his chair, turning his attention to the end of the table. Lady Forrester had sat the twins at the opposite ends of the table from him. He wouldn't be able to make conversation with Charlie unless he shouted. He caught Charlie's frown and offered her a smile of encouragement. His frustration didn't lie with her, but with her interfering guardian. Before Charlie could return his smile, Ralston turned on his charm. His flirtatious comment caused Charlie to giggle like the silly debutante she wasn't. It would be a long dinner if he had to endure watching Ralston flirt his way under Charlie's dress. At least Kincaid sat on her other side, and he had made his disinterest clear that afternoon.

"Charlotte looks exquisite this evening, does she not, Lord Sinclair?" asked Jacqueline.

"Exquisite is too tame of a word to describe Charlie." His eyes never strayed from the subject at hand.

"Lord Sinclair, you are looking at Evelyn. I believe Jacqueline mentioned Charlotte," stated Gemma.

"I am well aware of who we speak of, as are both of you." Sinclair glanced to his left and to his right before returning his stare upon Charlotte.

Both ladies laughed at his predicament, and that was how the rest of the dinner progressed for him. Each lady would take turns teasing him about Charlie while he watched Ralston flirt outrageously with her. The gentleman occupied her attention throughout dinner, and she never glanced his way again. Which only seemed to bring more amusement to his dinner partners. And Sinclair's frustration grew minute by agonizing minute.

Charlie was well aware of Jasper's stare throughout dinner. Many times she wanted to squirm in her seat at the intensity of it. Each stolen glance brought forth memories of their night together. Her body grew warm and an ache for him to kiss her consumed her thoughts. Every time she tried to get his attention, Jacqueline or Gemma would distract him. It would appear that Aunt Susanna wasn't the only family member who took pleasure from separating them. Each time Jacqueline or Gemma laughed, it was at the expense of Jasper. Charlie knew he held his frustration in check by the twitch of his eye. She had been on the receiving end of that twitch many times in the past when she pushed against him. He never reacted then, just as he wouldn't now. Instead, he would seek his revenge another way. And that Charlie took pleasure from. Now if only she could untangle herself from the disturbing conversation she kept having with Ralston. One that confused her. Why so late in the house party did he find Charlotte so interesting? At least Kincaid ignored her. Kincaid's behavior was disrespectful, but at this point Charlotte no longer cared. After all, it was a house party in the country, and the standard etiquette rules didn't apply. It was just one less person she had to convince as Evelyn.

"Your sister Charlotte looks lovely this evening. Her hair is quite fetching," said Ralston.

Charlie gave him a dumbfounded look when he wasn't looking. Did Ralston hear the rubbish coming out of his mouth? Polly styled Evelyn and Charlotte's hair the same way, even down to the color of the ribbon. They dressed similarly to confuse Worthington.

"Yes, she does. I also think my cousin Gemma looks stunning in her lavender dress."

Ralston glanced at Gemma, shrugged with indifference, then continued his perusal of Evelyn. While it would appear that he held no interest in Gemma, but for the briefest of seconds Charlie observed a longing in his glance. Then his mask of the rake he portrayed himself to be slipped back into place.

"Now your sister, she loves horses. Correct?"

"Yes, horses are Charlie's passion."

"Charlie?"

"Charlotte allows family members and close friends to call her Charlie."

"Mmm, I am sure I can become a close friend," Ralston murmured. "Does she know how to take care of the horses?"

Charlie sighed. "She would live in the stables if Uncle Theo gave her permission."

"Excellent."

"May I ask why the sudden interest in Charlotte? You have not spoken to her once during this house party."

"A neglect on my part, Lady Evelyn. I aim to remedy that as soon as I can. It has been ungentlemanly of me not to pay her notice."

"I do not mean to call attention to your lack of social niceties. I only wish to wonder why she draws your interest now."

"Well she is a feisty chit and I would love to …"

"Ralston," Kincaid growled. "You are talking to a lady."

"Oh, quite right. My apologies for my abrasive speech."

Charlotte waved her hand. Ralston still didn't answer why. "No need, my lord. Was there another reason?"

"Well, there is the offer …"

Kincaid once again stopped Ralston from answering any further. "Lady Evelyn, are you excited for your upcoming season in London? You must have your uncle take you to visit Hatchards, they have a wide selection of books to choose from."

Kincaid manipulated the remaining dinner conversation with his discussion of books stores in London, and Charlotte never got the chance to question Ralston further. If she were Evelyn, she would have taken great pleasure of learning of these treasure troves. But the conversation bored Charlotte to death. She smiled, nodded, and commented at all the appropriate openings in the conversation. When Aunt Susanna directed the ladies to the drawing room so that the gentlemen could drink their cognac and smoke their cigars, Charlie was never more grateful for dinner to end.

Charlie trailed behind the other ladies, hoping Jasper would talk to her. As she reached the drawing room, he pulled her into a dark alcove. Before she could tell him how much she missed him, he devoured her mouth, stealing kiss after kiss as if he were a man starving for a taste of her. When he lifted his head, he pulled her tight in his arms, holding her.

"I have missed you like crazy today."

"I woke up late. Evelyn made up a story of my being over-tired to cover for me. Then I had to lie about all day to appease Aunt Susanna," Charlie rambled on.

"You are well, though?"

Charlie beamed at Jasper. "Never better."

"Are you tender?" Jasper asked concerned.

"Only with pleasure."

"Mmm," Jasper murmured before slowly kissing her again.

Aunt Susanna stepped out of the drawing room, calling her name.

"I must return."

Jasper continued kissing along her neck. "Mmm."

When his hands lowered and pressed her against his cock, Charlie became muddled once again. His kisses hypnotized her only to the pleasure of Jasper. Then he started whispering seductively in her ear of the ways he wanted to worship her.

"I will find her, Aunt Susanna," said Evelyn.

Charlie untangled herself out of Jasper's embrace and stepped out of the alcove.

"I will be along shortly. The ribbon came undone on my slipper."

When Aunt Susanna and Evelyn seem satisfied with this, Jasper pulled her back into his arms. He placed a kiss on the nape of her neck.

"Meet me at midnight."

"I cannot get away."

"Forrester again?" Jasper growled.

Charlie heard the jealousy in Jasper's voice. She turned in his arms and placed a soft kiss on his lips. "No, my love. Jacqueline is being all parental with Evelyn and me. I cannot risk leaving the house."

Jasper sighed, "Please try."

Laura A. Barnes

Jasper desperately wanted to propose to Charlotte. If he didn't return to the gentlemen now, he wouldn't get the chance to propose. He would cause such a scandal that the whispers would spread across every home in England. Jasper stepped away and bowed before walking away.

Charlotte wished she could meet Jasper for another midnight rendezvous, but she'd promised her sisters that she wouldn't leave the house anymore at night while the house party was in full swing. However, the fingers she kept crossed behind her back when she promised didn't extend to sneaking into Jasper's bedroom later. She watched him, devouring his backside as he strolled away. Jasper's disappointment would only last for a short while.

Chapter Sixteen

Jasper wanted to slam the door to his bedroom in frustration. However, a gentleman never behaved rudely while a guest in another's home, especially a duke's home. The evening ended the way it began. He never got another moment alone with Charlotte. At every opportunity, a lady from her family would engage him in conversation, and he had to watch either Forrester, Ralston or Worthington manipulate her time. Worthington was a blind bloke who couldn't tell Evelyn or Charlie apart. That might have been comical to watch, if he wasn't so jealous of the gentlemen's time with Charlie.

Then, to end the evening on a sour note, he waited for Charlie at all her usual haunts on the estate. Jasper knew that Charlie made it clear she couldn't leave, but he still held out hope that she would find a way. When she didn't appear in the stable, he took the chance of riding to her favorite spot. No lantern highlighted her there with Forrester. Jasper even rode out to where they had made love the night before, hoping that she awaited him there. But there was no sign of Charlotte anywhere.

When he'd dressed that evening, he informed his valet to retire early for the evening. Jasper would undress himself. He slid his arms out of his suit jacket, sat on the bed, and yanked off his boots, throwing them on the rug. Before he untied his cravat, a pair of hands slid over his shoulders.

"Allow me," Charlotte whispered.

Jasper stilled, afraid that this was only an apparition. Once Charlie undid the garment, her fingers made quick work on the buttons of his shirt. When her hands slid down his chest, he moaned dropping his head back on her shoulder. He looked up into her eyes at her unspoken question.

"Kiss me, Charlotte."

"With pleasure," she sighed.

She lowered her head and placed the softest of kisses on Jasper's mouth. Her mouth opened above his and she traced his lips with her tongue. Softly stroking, urging him to open. When he did, she slipped inside and explored the flavor of Jasper. She savored the whiskey he drank with each stroke. At one time she hated the taste, now she only wanted to drink it from his lips all night.

Jasper's patience had worn past the point of no return. He turned and brought Charlie under him, taking over the kiss. His mouth demanded hers to match the passion that heated his soul. He located the ribbon around her robe and tore it loose. He wanted to rip the nightdress from her. Charlie surprised him. Jasper pulled back to gaze upon the woman who drove him crazy with desire. Charlotte wore not a stitch under the robe. She kept bringing every fantasy he had to life.

"Oh Charlie, my love, you are going to be the death of me."

She tilted her head in that maddening way. "Oh, I was trying for making you feel alive. If that is the case, perhaps I should return to my room." Charlie pushed at his chest for him to move. An impish smile gracing her face.

"You, my minx, are going nowhere."

"Well, I would hate for you to meet an untimely demise at my hands."

"I am only going to meet an untimely demise if your hands do not continue what they started."

"Far be it for me to be the reason for your untimely demise. How is this?" Charlie asked, her hand skimming down to brush across the placket of his trousers.

Jasper groaned, speechless at the caress.

With another tilt of her head, she said, "I am going to take your response as pleasurable. But sense I am unsure, perhaps if I do this, you will be more expressive."

Charlie undid his trousers and his cock sprang out. She wrapped her fingers around Jasper, stroking the length of his hardness. It was smooth and throbbed in her hand. Jasper growled and crushed his mouth down onto Charlie. The explosive kiss rocked Charlie to her core. He lowered his hand and joined hers. Jasper guided Charlie on how to please him. Their strokes grew bolder and his kisses continued to dominate Charlie's senses. Charlie felt the wetness between her thighs. Jasper hadn't even touched her and her ache begged for release. She wanted to crawl inside him and be one with Jasper.

Jasper needed to be inside Charlie now. Her sense perfumed the air with her need. He pulled her hands away from him and held them above her head. When her legs wrapped around his waist and she pressed her wetness against his cock, he took her in one thrust. Her body arched off the bed into him. Jasper couldn't be gentle with Charlie even if he wanted to. His body had ached for her since they parted the night before. With each stroke, he drew her soul into his.

Charlie's body left her and flowed into Jasper's. She matched him stroke for stroke, never wanting Jasper to stop this madness. If this was what loving somebody with your whole heart felt like, then she never wanted it to end. Jasper released her hands, and she pressed her body tighter against him. Her nipples tightened against his rough chest. His hands gripped her waist, leaving his mark on her. Not only on her body, but on her soul. Charlie's body tightened before it spiraled out of control.

Jasper took them flying over the edge with each thrust. When Charlie came apart in his arms, he caught and held her close while they soared with pleasure. Jasper closed his eyes, drawing in a deep breath before he settled with Charlie clinging to him. Their bodies locked into an embrace they never wanted to be released from.

They lay for an endless amount of time, before Charlie propped herself on Jasper's chest. She traced his face with her fingertips, her touch lingering over the small scar above his eyebrow.

"I never meant to harm you that day."

Jasper opened his eyes to Charlie's frown. "I know, my love, and anyway I deserved it."

"No, you did not. I let my temper get the better of me."

"One that I provoked."

"Why did you?"

Jasper sighed, "You were under my skin even then. I just did not realize the full impact. When Gray suggested that we settle our differences with swords, I underestimated your skill with the weapon. I never imagined you would hold your own against me. However, you proved me wrong." Jasper rolled them over, placing a kiss on Charlie's lips. "Also, this scar reminds me to never turn my back on you." Jasper laughed.

"I would not mind if you choose to do so on occasion," whispered Charlie, running her hands along the backside of Jasper.

"You minx," Jasper growled.

Jasper closed his eyes at Charlotte's touch. As much as he wanted to keep her in his bed all night, he must get her back to her bedroom before anyone noticed she was missing.

"I thought you could not meet me at midnight. What made you change your mind?" asked Jasper.

"I told you I could not meet you *outside* the house. I never mentioned we could not meet *inside* the house."

"You led me to believe we would not meet at all."

"I wanted to surprise you. Were you?"

"Mmm, very much so. Your appearance in my room relieved my frustration."

"Why were your frustrated?"

"Because I spent the past few hours waiting for you outside at your tree, then at the stables, then at the pond where we first made love, back to your tree again. I had hoped you would appear. But much to my disappointment, you never arrived. With a heavy heart, I returned to my room. A rejected suitor disappointed with his conquest."

"You tell a tall tale, Sinclair. I almost hold sympathy for you, except that I know how your evening ended. Are you still disappointed with your conquest?" Charlie fluttered her eyelashes.

"Mmm no, my lady. If anything, I am enamored of her even more so."

Jasper went from teasing to charming in a matter of seconds. Charlie's heart softened to a puddle of mush. "Did you really search for me?"

Jasper nodded.

"Why?"

This was his moment to propose. To profess his undying love to Charlotte. But he didn't. Everything he wanted to say to Charlie froze on the tip of Jasper's tongue. There would never be a more perfect opportunity than having her lie in his embrace. However, it was not perfect. Charlotte deserved the grand gesture. She deserved to believe that he wanted her regardless of their lovemaking. She deserved a romantic proposal in a perfect setting that would always conjure enjoyable memories. And Jasper knew where and when he would propose. In the meantime, he would woo her with whatever charming regard he possessed.

"Why to steal more kisses from your lips," answered Jasper, claiming her mouth to prove his intentions.

Charlie melted under Jasper's attention, sighing after every sweet kiss. Even though a small part of her had wanted Jasper to confess his undying love. She had thought he might even propose. Did she misunderstand his feelings for her? Did he only consider their time a way to slack his lust or did he love her? Questions that Charlie was too afraid to ask for fear of his answer. Still, her doubts didn't keep her from responding to his kisses. They only made her want to capture every moment with Jasper. Even if he would break her heart. In which Charlie still held belief that he wouldn't.

"Love, we must get you back to your room."

Charlie pouted.

Jasper laughed and lay back, resting his arms behind his head. "Unless, you wish to stay the night."

Charlie swatted at Jasper. "You know I cannot. Why do you tease me?"

"Because I enjoy the spark in your eyes when I do."

"You are incorrigible, Jasper Sinclair."

"Only for you, Charlotte Holbrooke."

"If you say so," answered Charlie, rising from the bed.

Jasper groaned at the sight of Charlie in the moonlight. The picture of a goddess. With her hair hanging to her waist, the glow of the moon shimmered across her breasts, lighting a trail of light across her body. The brief flashes emphasized the darkness of her curves. Curves he ached to caress throughout the night into the early dawn. When Charlie covered herself with a robe, disappointment settled once again in Jasper. Even while he held Charlie within his grasp, they were still kept apart.

Jasper sat on the edge of the bed. He reached out to draw Charlie onto his knee. "I do," he murmured, kissing her neck. "Now, how do we return you to your bedroom undetected?"

"Through the secret passageway," Charlie whispered.

"This estate holds a secret passageway?"

Charlie nodded. A mischievous smile lit her face.

"I never knew."

"It is a family secret."

"Then that explains …"

Charlie winced, and wore a guilty expression.

The secret passage explained the odd occurrences Jasper faced the other times he had stayed overnight. Every visit when he awakened in the morning, a piece of his clothing would be missing. Then he would find an animal on the estate wearing it. Every time his valet would stutter in embarrassment that he held no clue on who pranked him. While Jasper always held a suspicion that it was Charlie, he never proved it. Even when her entire family laughed at his expense, they never revealed her as the culprit.

"Do you forgive me?"

"Are you even sorry for your actions?"

Charlie laughed, "No, you deserved every bit of my retaliation."

"So I did. Shall we call a truce, my dear?"

"An offer I shall have to consider."

"When might you have an answer? Or will I have to always wait on guard for your next plan of attack?"

"I shall give you my answer tomorrow at lunch."

"That will be awkward in front of all the guests."

"That is where you are wrong. Tomorrow's luncheon holds a surprise for you."

"How so?"

"I cannot tell you now. Aunt Susanna is announcing her plans at breakfast. So you must get some sleep, you do not want to sleep until noon again," Charlie replied cheekily, walking to the mirror on the wall.

"Well, when a certain wench keeps me awake all hours of the night, a man must rest until noon to regain his strength."

"Yes, one your age must get all the sleep he can get."

"Charlie," Jasper growled.

"Kiss me good night, Jasper."

"With pleasure."

Jasper drew Charlotte in his arms and kissed her with all the passion he possessed. When she sighed and melted in his arms, Jasper pressed his hardness into her to prove his stamina. Charlie wrapped herself tighter around him, clinging to his shoulders. Her whimpers, when he flicked his thumb across her nipple, brought a smile of satisfaction to his face. Jasper took pleasure from how he affected Charlie. With reluctance, he pulled away.

"Off to bed, wench."

Charlie pressed the decorative gilding around the mirror. The mirror swung open, revealing a dark passageway. Jasper stuck his head inside, glancing back and forth. He frowned with displeasure that Charlie had risked herself to see him. Jasper walked to the nightstand and lit the candle.

Charlie waited for Jasper to lecture her on the unsafe passageway. In the dark, it looked ominous. Although it was anything but. When one wanted to travel through the passageway, they only had to light a candle and a smooth path would await them. Uncle Theo kept the walkway clean and safe. He encouraged the girls to use it during the night, if they wanted to go to each other's rooms or to visit the library. He thought it would keep them from becoming compromised if caught alone while they had guests. However, her uncle wouldn't approve of her usage of it this evening.

When they stepped into the passageway, the cleanliness of it surprised Jasper. There were no old creaking boards or cobwebs clinging to the walls. He even caught a whiff of beeswax and lemon. The path shined the same as the hallways in the estate. Still, he didn't much care for Charlie venturing to meet him this way. Now wasn't the time to scold her. He didn't want to risk anyone catching them sneaking around. Instead, Jasper held Charlie's hand, guiding them along the narrow passage. Charlie tugged on his hand, prompting him to stop. She angled her head toward the wall and he realized they had reached her room.

With a quick kiss, Charlie maneuvered the mechanism to allow her access back inside her bedroom. Once she slipped inside, Jasper walked back to his room. While the passage might have been clean, it gave off an eerie sense. Not to mention strange noises echoing around him. Once he reached his door, he sighed with relief. Jasper blew out his candle and had been about to shut the trap door, when he heard footsteps coming from where he had returned. At first he thought Charlie was returning to him, but as the steps grew closer, he heard the heavy footfall of a man. Jasper peeked out through the small opening, and Kincaid surprised him when he strolled past.

It would appear that Jasper wasn't the only gentleman ruining one of Colebourne's wards. The question remained; which lady had Kincaid set his sights on? And would he offer for the miss? Without knowing which bedroom Kincaid visited, Sinclair wouldn't know which girl Kincaid should offer for. Sinclair would have to be more observant in the next couple of days. So far, he had yet to see Kincaid pay interest to any of the ladies in attendance. However, since he came from the family side of the estate, it had to be one of them. Jasper ruled out Charlotte. And Evelyn too, since her heart was set on Worthington. Which only left Jacqueline, Gemma, or Abigail. There wasn't much he could do now except to step in the passageway and confront Kincaid. But that would only draw suspicion toward Charlotte and himself. Something he wished to avoid at all costs.

Chapter Seventeen

Lady Forrester observed the interaction between the guests. So far the house party had been a success, and they still had two days remaining to make matches between the girls. They had done her proud, acting the perfect ladies. Especially Charlotte. Theo and her worried over Charlie's behavior, since any other time her unlady-like qualities made them cringe. However, the attention Lord Sinclair paid Charlotte must have affected the girl. Even now the sly glances they exchanged didn't go unnoticed. Susanna sensed the lord would propose before the end of the ball. Theo mentioned Sinclair's fury at the enticement dangled amongst the bachelors for Charlotte's hand. If Sinclair didn't come to scratch, then there were other bachelors who would. However, that would only cause heartbreak amongst the other girls. For the other ladies already had their hearts set on certain gentlemen. So, today's picnic would be about setting the perfect scene to bring these couples together.

Susanna clinked her spoon against a glass to draw attention. She smiled at the guests. "For today's activities, I have planned a picnic near the lake on the south part of the estate. This, my lovely guests, will be no ordinary picnic. Each couple will enjoy their own picnic basket. There are blankets scattered around and baskets filled with each girl's choosing. They will be waiting for each gentleman to join them for an entertaining afternoon. Once the gentleman arrives at the destination, I will direct you to the lady who drew your name. There are many excellent pathways for walking, boats to take out on the lake, and a gorgeous afternoon to enjoy."

Once Jasper caught Charlotte's gaze, she winked at him. This must have been the surprise she teased him about. Even though they would be under watchful eyes, Jasper would still spend time in Charlotte's company. He assumed with the wink he was Charlotte's chosen gentleman. He only hoped he was the chosen gentleman in more ways than one.

~~~~~

When Sinclair and the other gentlemen arrived on horseback at the afternoon destination, it was to find each lady waiting on a blanket, each place a respectable yet private distance. Charlotte, dressed in a yellow creation that contradicted her innocence, drew Sinclair's eyes. The allure of what lay underneath all that silk heightened Sinclair's desire for the chit. What he wouldn't do to be alone with Charlie in the open fields. He wanted to strip her naked and make love to her all afternoon. While he imagined how he would love Charlie, he didn't hear Lady Forrester calling his name.

"Lord Sinclair?"

After the fog lifted, Sinclair glanced around to see the other gentlemen shaking their heads at him in disgust, while the ladies sighed. Sinclair had made a spectacle of himself by focusing his gaze on Charlotte. Charlotte made him lose all rational thought whenever she was near.

"Yes?"

Lady Forrester smirked. "Charlotte drew your name. You may join her for luncheon."

Sinclair looked like a fool, but he didn't care. He couldn't wipe the silly grin from his face, even if he tried. He didn't even want to. Sinclair strolled over to Charlie and bowed. Charlie tried to hold her laughter in, but failed.

She released not a silly giggle, but a full-blown laugh from the belly that made her cry.

"It would appear I am the lucky gentleman who gets to enjoy your companionship this afternoon. You are a lovely vision of sunshine today, Lady Charlotte."

Charlotte lifted a hand where he placed a kiss across her knuckles. Before anyone noticed, he slid his tongue between her fingers, softly stroking. With a gasp, Charlie's laughter stopped. Only for her to release the same sigh she used when he gave her pleasure. The blush spreading across her cheeks only heightened the desire swirling around them. Desire they couldn't act upon. However, it wouldn't stop Sinclair from skirting the edge of propriety. Yes, it would be a lovely afternoon.

The heat of Jasper's touch had Charlie squirming. If he didn't sit down soon, it would only draw more attention their way. Attention Jasper had caused with his scandalous gaze when he first arrived. He almost caused a spectacle in the way he regarded her. The way he still regarded her even now.

"Please sit, Lord Sinclair, so we can enjoy our lunch."

Charlotte swept a hand to show him where to sit. However, Jasper rested his back against the tree, with one leg extended and the other bent to prop his arm on. Charlie sat near the tree for shade. If looked too close upon by the other guests, they would whisper that Jasper and Charlie sat indecently close. Charlie gestured for Jasper to slide over. The maddening man shook his head and remained where he was. Charlotte glanced around, and to her relief no one paid them any attention.

"Do you know how much I wish I could kiss you at this moment?" Jasper asked.

"Shh."

"And how much I wish I could make love to you under the open skies?"

"My lord, would you care for some ..."

"Kisses?"

"Jasper, please hush. Someone will hear you."

Jasper laughed. "No one is paying us the least bit of attention. They are all caught up in their own drama." He stretched out to touch his fingers to hers.

Charlie curled her fingers around his, glancing around at the other guests. Jacqueline ate with Kincaid, and neither of them talked. Evelyn was paired with Worthington. They also didn't talk. Charlie frowned. She wished her sisters were experiencing the same happiness as herself, but it wasn't to be. She could tell Evelyn was near tears at Worthington's disregard. Charlie had to find some way to bring them together. Gemma had drawn Lord Ralston's name. The rake flirted with her cousin. The most comical was Duncan and Selina. Selina glared at her partner, but Duncan only grinned and kept popping grapes into his mouth, while listening to her tirade at being stuck with him. She looked amongst the other couples, searching for Abigail. Charlie found her arguing near the woods with Lucas. Lucas held Abigail's arm in his grasp. When she shook him off, Abigail ran off into the woods, and Lucas followed. Charlie tried to rise, but Sinclair stopped her.

"Leave them be."

"But ..."

"Charlotte, do not interfere in something you do not understand."

"I understand that my friend loves my cousin, and my cousin is too pigheaded to realize how special Abigail is."

"I think he realizes it, he just will not admit to it."

"Humph."

"Charlie, shall we focus on us? Like how much I missed you in my bed after you left."

"Jasper, please stop speaking so wickedly."

"Why? I love making you blush. Now, shall we eat or do I need to find another blanket to sit upon?"

"You are exasperating like always."

"My dear, we may have taken our relationship to a more intimate level, but how I treat you will never change."

"Never?" Charlie asked, sliding a hand along the length of his thigh.

"Mmm, never."

"That is a shame," said Charlie, leaning over Jasper to reach the basket.

Jasper gulped at the low neckline to Charlie's dress. When she reached across him, her dress gaped open, giving him a view of her swollen breasts. Charlie pulled back, so slowly that her body brushed across his intimately. When she settled back, her seductive smile would have brought him to his knees if he weren't seated already

"Um, what is a shame?" Jasper lost track of the conversation.

"That you will treat me no different, even though you have taken my innocence and ruined me so scandalously," Charlie answered with a cheeky grin.

"I think you are the one who has ruined me for any other woman."

"Who, me?"

"You know damn well the affect you have over me, Charlotte Holbrooke. I would show you now, if so many people did not surround us," Jasper growled.

Charlie threw back her head and laughed. Soon she had their plates filled with every decadent treat. Jasper should have known Charlie would fill their lunch basket with nothing but sugar. Her sweet tooth had always been her demise. After eating cake, biscuits, cream puffs, and jam-filled pastries, Jasper laid back and closed his eyes. Charlie's voice was mesmerizing as she talked about Sapphire. Their love of horses was something they held in common. Charlie's excitement for Sapphire's new foal was contagious. He had almost drifted asleep when a commotion near the pond had him jumping to his feet.

Selina was trudging out of the water with Forrester's assistance. The lady's hair lay in a soaked décor with her ribbons hanging over her face. She swiped them away in annoyance, holding up the heavy skirt to step over the rocks. The once pristine white dress now hung on Selina stained a mucky brown. Moss clung to the buttons, and she appeared to be missing a shoe.

"You utter buffoon. Look what you have done to my dress," Selina shrieked at Forrester.

"A simple accident, my lady. I apologize for my unsteadiness."

"You stood up in the boat, tipping it over. That is not an accident."

"Only for the purpose of swatting away a bee you were caterwauling about."

"Caterwauling! I do not lower myself to that tone. I only whimpered when the insect landed on my parasol."

Forrester guffawed. "Believe me, your response was no whimper."

"Your manners, sir, leave a lot to be desired. You are nothing but an over-large, uncoordinated, disrespectable excuse for a gentleman."

"Well, you are no lady yourself."

"Well, I …" Selina stomped a foot at his audacity. He made her so angry, she couldn't form the words to describe his true character. "Grhh."

Selina stomped away to her father to garner sympathy. Her father helped her into a curricle and they rode back to the house for her to change clothes. And probably to sulk. Since Duncan had embarrassed Selina, she would be on the warpath to make someone more miserable than her. And since Abigail had been paired with Lucas and not her, then reason said Selina would strike out at Abigail. Charlie would need to stay close to Abigail once they returned to the house. Not that Abigail needed protection, she could hold her own, usually more with kindness than anything else. Still, Charlie wanted to offer support, and she knew her sisters and Gemma would feel no different.

Droplets flew through the air when Duncan shook his body. He'd lost his hat when he went under and tried to save the ungrateful lass. His red locks lay drenched with the rest of his clothing. However, he would endure it all over again to catch the sight of a soaked lass. A soaked lass no matter how angry leaves nothing to the imagination. A soaked lass only fuels fantasies that one would want to act upon if given a chance. Selina made a very fine soaked lass indeed.

Duncan plopped down on an empty spot on Charlie and Sinclair's blanket. He dug around in their basket, pulling out a slice of chocolate cake. Duncan tore into the treat, finishing it in three bites.

He heard Sinclair mutter, "Savage" before sitting back down.

"I should have known you were the one who came away with all the sweets," said Duncan, digging through the basket for more to eat. "The wench who packed my lunch served me nothing but what a rabbit would eat."

"Oh, you poor man."

Duncan raised his head to wink at Charlie's teasing tone. He caught her staring at his bare legs covered in slime. Duncan also saw Sinclair's possessive stare of Charlie and knew the gent didn't care for her notice of him. Duncan wanted to have a little fun at Sinclair's expense.

"Like what you see, lass?" Duncan asked, raising his eyebrows.

Charlie shrugged, raking her gaze up and down Duncan's length. "Not bad, but a little too hairy for my taste." Charlie wrinkled her nose.

Sinclair growled a warning, but Duncan ignored it. He was no threat to Sinclair's courtship of Charlie, but the bloke didn't need to know that yet.

"Do you recall that matter I discussed with you the other night?"

"Yes," answered Charlie.

"Well, it might have progressed further than I anticipated."

"Duncan, how could you? Do you not understand the repercussions this will cause?"

"A heart does not see the reason the mind understands."

"You are a fool."

"Only for you, Charlie, my girl."

Charlie laughed, warmed by Duncan's flirtation. Since she knew it was harmless gibberish, she didn't pay any attention to what Sinclair might interpret it to be.

"Can I assume your situation has progressed further too?"

Charlie blushed. "Yes, it has."

Duncan glared at Sinclair, assessing Sinclair's reaction to his conversation with Charlie. The gentleman's jealousy satisfied Duncan. If the man grew agitated at a simple interchange, then it meant he cared for Charlie. Duncan would do nothing to stand in their way.

"Excellent. We shall talk later." Duncan jumped up, extending his hand to Sinclair. "I am withdrawing from the duke's offer."

Sinclair warily shook Forrester's hand and nodded. Even though he didn't trust the Scot. His familiarity with Charlie still bothered him. Then there was Charlie's open perusal of Forrester in his kilt. Their flirty exchange didn't help appease his jealously. He wondered how Charlie would feel if he flirted with another woman. Would she be just as jealous?

Sinclair shook his head. There was no other lady he wanted to charm than the one sitting next to him. Nor did he want to play games. Charlie insisted Forrester was only her friend, and he trusted her. So instead of letting past doubts fester, he needed to let them go.

"Shall we walk this delightful lunch off?" asked Sinclair.

Charlie beamed at Jasper. His open acceptance to her quirky ways warmed her heart. Any other gentleman would have lectured her on eating too many sweets. Instead, Jasper indulged her weaknesses.

"I would enjoy that very much."

By then the other couples had finished their lunches and were partaking in the many outdoor activities provided for them. Jasper led them along a path around the lake. They would stop to skip a few rocks, then continue until they were far enough away where nobody noticed when he led them into the wooded area nearby.

Once they had ventured deep enough, Jasper backed Charlie against a tree. His seductive smile spoke of his intentions. Intentions Charlie wouldn't object to, for she had patiently waited all day for them. However, Jasper didn't place his lips on hers. He started his assault placing soft kisses across her chest, trailing higher along her neck. When he reached her lips, Jasper hesitated but a breath away, driving Charlie's anticipation up a notch. His stare at her lips hypnotized her. His eyes darkening with a desire he hadn't shown before. Charlie drew her bottom lip through her teeth.

Charlie's eagerness showed for his kiss. His thumb smoothed out her teeth from her bottom lip. Sliding it back and forth over the smooth expanse. How he wanted to sample her sweetness, savor the raspberry jam flavor he knew she would taste like. Instead, his lips trailed back down her neck, nipping at her silky skin.

"Jasper," Charlie moaned.

"Mmm."

"Are you going to kiss me?"

"No," he whispered. His tongue dipping inside the front of her dress.

"No?"

"No." He pulled away, sauntering back out of the woods near the lake.

Charlie stood frustrated against the tree. She had hoped when he detoured them into the woods, Jasper would kiss her. Instead, he only heightened her desire to a level of frustration that he would deny. Not only that, Charlie also noticed his smile when he walked away. He took pleasure from withholding his kisses. Perhaps she was wrong. Jasper's display proved his comment of remaining the arrogant arse he had always been to her. If that was the case, then she would remain the hoyden when provoked by him to act before she thought through her actions.

She stalked out of the woods to find him near the lake with his foot propped on a rock. When he didn't turn at her arrival, she let her vindictive nature shine by shoving him into the lake. Then Charlotte stood with her hands on her hips, glaring at him when he surfaced. When he broke out in laughter at her display of revenge, she lowered her hands and stomped her foot.

"My dear, if you wanted to see my body dripping with water again, you only had to make your request known and I would have obliged your desires."

"As if you knew how to oblige a lady's desires."

"Mmm, I am sure you would find many to disagree with you, including yourself," Jasper taunted.

"Why?"

Jasper came out of the water, pausing but an inch from Charlie. Her fury at denying her a kiss rolled off her in waves. He loved watching her like this. Their marriage would never be boring. Granted, he would have to spend many nights making up for the times he would anger her. They would be pleasurable. However, now he had to make it appear that nothing untoward went on when he steered them into the woods. He had to leave when he did, if not he would have taken her against the tree. His need for Charlie consumed him so much, he forgot about her reputation. When she looked at him with so much trust and vulnerability, he froze.

"Why what?"

"Why did you not kiss me?" Charlie hissed.

"Because once I started with one kiss, then it would turn to two, then three, then I would never have been able to stop," Jasper whispered.

"Oh …"

Jasper smiled at Charlie tenderly. "Yes, oh."

"I am sorry?" Charlie winced.

"Are you stating your apology or asking?"

"Both?"

Before the crowd gathered, Jasper spoke softly, "You may seek your forgiveness later."

Charlie gulped when she realized Jasper's underlying message.

Aunt Susanna pulled Charlie to the side to lecture her on the inappropriate behavior of young ladies. While listening to her, Charlie's gaze kept drifting to Jasper. Where he sent her smoldering stares, stating exactly what he expected for an apology. If the sun warmed Charlie before, the heat burned her now. Inside and out. That was the force of Jasper Sinclair. Nothing but a fire that never sizzled out.

Chapter Eighteen

Dinner was a quiet affair. Most of the ladies pleaded too much sun from the afternoon and took a tray in their rooms for dinner. Since most of the chaperones and Aunt Susanna herself didn't go to dinner, Uncle Theo thought it would be best for what girls who wanted dinner to have a small affair in the upstairs parlor. The gentlemen decided to take dinner at the inn in town, and to visit the taverns for a few drinks.

Charlie stood at the window looking for any sign of Jasper's return. The other ladies discussed amongst themselves their dresses for tomorrow's ball. She smiled over her shoulder when they laughed about the afternoon. Over the course of the last few days, they had formed new friendships. Friendships that would be beneficial when they arrived in London for the season. Charlie thought Jasper would have proposed by now. Since he hadn't, Charlie had to face the music that he might not. If that were the case, then she would need to find herself a husband in London. It was the pact the girls had decided when they agreed to the house party. They worried over Uncle Theo, and they owed him to make matches so he wouldn't have to worry over them anymore. Her uncle was a generous soul, and Charlie loved him like a father. A father who overindulged her over the years with horses and her rebellious character. One who spoiled all of them in their own unique way.

The sound of horses drew Charlie's attention back outside, but it was only Kincaid and Worthington returning. With a sigh of disappointment, Charlie returned to the settee to join the discussion. She wasn't one to fawn over the fashion plates, but even Charlie's excitement over her gown that arrived from London this afternoon was hard to contain. It was a work of creation that stunned Charlie. She waited in anticipation for Jasper to see it.

"Well, if this is not another quaint gathering. At least the gentlemen have left for the evening. It would be a shame for any of them to witness your drab garb."

Selina stood in the doorway, dressed in an elegant day dress with her claws out. She looked down at her nose at them. The humiliation from her earlier drowning would play no effectiveness in her shrew comments.

"Our invitation for you to join us is still open," said Abigail.

Selina sneered, "As if I would want to join your little party. You ladies are ranked below me and will always be lower than my status. Once I am a duchess, your comfortable situations will change. I will not allow you to remain living here for free. The dukedom has paid for your welfare long enough. My advice to you wards is to find a man to marry tomorrow night or during your season in London. Because after you have your London season, Lucas and I are getting married. I will not be as generous as your uncle and neither will Lucas."

Throughout Selina's tirade she had stepped further into the room, landing in front of Abigail. While she meant her words for all of them, she targeted Abigail with her harshness. Charlie noticed the sadness in Abigail's eyes, but her friend wouldn't allow Selina Pemberton to cower her. Abigail pressed her shoulders back and held her head high. Abigail didn't mince words with the shrew, instead returning her gaze with a determination

Charlie had never witnessed in Abigail. Before Abigail spoke her opinion, a voice from the doorway stopped Selina's vindictiveness.

"Presumptuous, are you not, Lady Selina?" drawled Duncan, leaning on the doorjamb.

"No, I do not believe I am, Lord Forrester," Selina replied snidely, turning toward him.

"Have you and Lucas set a wedding date?"

"Papa and the duke will set the date once the house party has completed and the guests have left."

"So, nothing is set in stone *per se.*"

"It has been set in stone since Lucas and I were children."

"Perhaps, but a stone can be broken, just as your betrothal can."

"There are no grounds on which it can break."

"Isn't there?"

Selina turned pale at Duncan's taunt. Was there more to Duncan's involvement with Selina than the mere kiss they shared in the hallway?

"You, my lord, are overstepping your bounds as usual," snarled Selina. She gathered her skirts, and turning she tried to exit the room. Before she left Duncan grabbed her wrist and pulled her to him. He lowered his head and whispered in Selina's ear. Selina pulled her hand away to slap Duncan. Duncan cocked an eyebrow and made a small shake with his head. Selina growled unlady-like and stomped away.

Duncan faced the ladies and made a bow. "I hope you ladies have enjoyed your leisurely evening resting. Because tomorrow evening I expect all you ladies to accept my offer for a twirl around the ballroom."

Charlie shook her head at Duncan's charm. While his flirtation held no effect on her or the rest of her family, it did on the other ladies. They twittered their responses, causing Duncan to become more obnoxious.

"Have all the gentlemen returned from the village?" asked Jacqueline.

"Yes, we returned earlier than expected."

"How so? Did someone fall ill?" asked Gemma.

"More like a gentlemanly disagreement ensued, and the villagers requested that they return to the estate to settle their differences."

"What kind of disagreement?" asked Charlie.

"I can only say that it involved winning a prize at the end of the house party?"

"What kind of prize?" asked Evelyn.

"A prize between gentlemen regarding a bet of sorts. You know how gentlemen can be."

"Foolish," Abigail muttered loud enough for everyone to hear.

"Foolish indeed." Duncan agreed. "Now, I must bid you good evening. I wish you all pleasant dreams."

Duncan walked around the room and kissed every lady's hand before leaving. After Duncan left, the other ladies oohed and awed over his attention. Charlie wanted to roll her eyes at their adoration of Duncan. While she didn't fall for his charm, Charlie understood how other ladies who didn't know him would. That was Duncan's flaw. He charmed them until they were falling at his feet, then when they wanted more, he fled so fast in the opposite direction they could never catch him even if they wanted to.

~~~~~~

Once Evelyn's light snores filled the bedroom, Charlie slipped out of bed, drawing on her robe. Leaving their room two nights in a row was risky, but one she could explain to Evelyn if caught. This time wasn't for herself, but for a friend. Duncan's mood didn't fool her. She had noticed an underlying tension in him after his interaction with Selina. He'd slipped a note in her hand when he kissed her good evening, and she knew it was a request to meet him later. Charlie lit a candle and held the note under the light.

Use the secret corridor and meet in my room at midnight.

Duncan didn't address or sign the note. The need for secrecy would protect them both as long as she didn't get caught in his bedroom. Charlie would make the visit quick, then return to her bed. She didn't even want to visit Jasper again. His behavior at the picnic still sat sour with her. Jasper's nonchalant regard to the change in their relationship upset her. Charlie expected Jasper to treat her differently. Didn't she deserve to have him treat her special? Especially since he loved her. But did he? Jasper had yet to speak any words of love, and Charlie didn't know if he ever would.

Charlie slipped out of the narrow opening, keeping it slightly ajar so as not to awaken Evelyn when she returned. Once she reached Duncan's bedroom, she used their special knock. Duncan opened the door and pulled her through, then he covered her mouth before she screamed at his rough treatment.

"Hush for a few minutes. If I let you go, will you stay quiet?"

Charlie nodded and Duncan released her. He wrapped Charlie in a quilt and led her to the farthest part of his room, away from any openings. Then he went back and pressed his ear against the secret door. After he seemed confident no one would disturb them, he returned to Charlie, sprawling in the chair before the fire. He lifted a bottle of whiskey and drank deeply. After Duncan finished, he held the bottle out to Charlie.

"No, thank you."

"Suit yourself."

"What was so urgent that I had to sneak out to you?"

"You've never questioned meeting before. Why now?"

"Because I promised Jacqueline that for the rest of the house party I would behave properly."

"Was this before or after you shoved Sinclair into the lake?"

"After," Charlie mumbled.

"Why the act of defiance?"

"Because."

"Because why?" Duncan persisted.

"Because he treated me like the pompous arse he always used to be."

"And was this before or after you snuck away into the woods?"

"Both. You saw?"

Duncan nodded.

"Did anyone else?"

Duncan shrugged.

Charlie started pacing back and forth. "If they did, someone would have spoken up. Or are they waiting to gossip at tomorrow's ball?" Charlie's whisper grew louder with every step.

Duncan grabbed Charlie and planted her back onto the chair. "You must stay quiet before someone catches us and they force us to wed. There has been an unusual amount of traffic in the passageway this evening. We cannot risk getting caught."

"What am I to do?"

Duncan sighed, realizing that he would have to discuss Charlie's dilemma before she would help him with his. He didn't even understand his own complicated problem.

"Tell me about Sinclair's treatment toward you."

"While we ate, he implied that just because our relationship had changed, he would treat me no different."

"Why should he?"

"Why should he not?"

"Keep explaining."

"Then he guided me back into the woods. Tempted me with … you know."

"Tempted?"

"With a kiss, but then turned and left before kissing me. Why even attempt to get us alone, if he was only going to leave?"

"Charlie, my girl, you do not understand how a man's mind works."

"How would I? Uncle Theo has always been attentive and spoils us to no end. Lucas is like a brother, protective yet understanding, sometimes anyway. And you are like a girl's best friend."

"Flatterer."

Charlie frowned at Duncan.

"You scare Sinclair. He realizes that he not only has to look out for himself, but also you too. His behavior today displayed how he tried to protect your honor. When he arrived at the picnic and blatantly undressed you with his eyes, he noticed the attention he drew. So he needed to revert to his old behavior to draw the attention off you. Then, like a fool, he snuck you into the woods. His conscience must have spoken, so he left you wondering. Which is never a good thing to do with you. Because your mind conjures incorrect reasons for his behavior. Hence pushing him into the pond."

Charlie winced. Perhaps she had taken this afternoon a little overboard. Jasper muddled with her mind as usual. She never even took into consideration that he might have been protecting her.

"I understand now."

"Good."

"Duncan?"

"Yes."

"Before we discuss why I am here, can you tell me about the scuffle in the village?"

"'Tis nothing. Just a disagreement between three gentlemen."

"Which three gentlemen?"

"Worthington, Ralston, and Sinclair."

"About?"

"Just a silly wager Uncle mentioned. Ralston had too much to drink and baited the other two."

"What is the wager?"

"Nothing, just a gentleman's bet. Nothing more."

Charlie shrugged in acceptance. If it were something important, she trusted that Duncan would tell her. Since he didn't elaborate, it must be something ridiculous. Most bets were between gentlemen. However, boys will be boys.

"Just one more question. What did you mean by unusual activity in the passageway this evening?"

"I have heard footsteps walking up and down while I waited for you. Once when I peeked out, thinking it was you. I noticed Sinclair wandering the hallway. How would Sinclair have knowledge of the passageway?"

"I might have paid him a visit last night …"

Duncan closed his eyes. When he opened them he glared at her. "Are you mad?"

"Perhaps a little."

"If Sinclair does not have a ring on your finger by the end of the ball, then whatever Uncle Theo decides on your fate, I will support."

"Even if it is not Sinclair?"

"Even if it is not Sinclair."

"You are being unfair."

"No, I am being reasonable. The man cannot ruin you and not marry you. If he does not, then the man does not deserve you."

"He will."

"Humph."

"Now onto your problem, Duncan. What is so dire?"

"I might have compromised Lady Selina."

"Might have?"

"Not completely, but my actions might have progressed too far."

"Uncle Theo will have your head, not to mention what Lucas might do."

"Do you not think I know that?" Duncan growled, rising to his feet to pace back and forth. Something he reprimanded Charlie for he now did himself.

"Sit," Charlie hissed.

Duncan sat on the edge of the chair, running his hands through his hair. He kept tapping his foot, showing his agitation. He realized the predicament he'd put himself in. At first it had been a distraction to forget his troubles from back home. Then Selina got under his skin like she always did. Before this trip he could ignore the temptation, convincing himself that she was too high in the instep for him. Then there was the matter of Selina being promised to his cousin. On this trip, there had been a shift that he couldn't quite explain. Was it because Selina would marry Lucas in a matter of months?

Selina Pemberton was the complete opposite of what he desired in a lady. She was too haughty, vindictive to his loved ones, a spoiled brat. One that he wanted to tame. Because under all her bitchiness was a lonely lady who only wanted someone to love her. Her attitude was nothing but a protective barrier that she kept shrouded in ice. Ice that melted at his touch. Duncan loved Lucas like a brother, but Lucas didn't deserve Selina. He did.

"Do you care for Selina?"

"Yes."

Charlie grimaced. "Why?"

"I cannot even explain it to myself, let alone to you."

"I understand."

"What am I to do?"

"You need to convince Selina to call off the betrothal."

"That will not be an option."

"Did you ask her?"

"I tried, but you see I am not her cup of tea. Her scathing words were along the lines of why would she marry a Scottish heathen when she will eventually be a duchess."

"She has a point," Charlie teased.

"Grr, another bleedin' female with not a sympathetic heart."

"Duncan, where Selina Pemberton is concerned there is no such emotion."

"There is more to her. You only see what she wants you to see."

"A matter we shall never agree on. Maybe you're attracted to Selina, because you see her as a challenge."

"How so?"

"Because any lady you encounter falls at your feet for attention. Selina does not. You, my friend, enjoy the chase. The question is; once you catch Selina, will you feel the same way? Or will the excitement wear off?"

Duncan pondered Charlie's comment. Was that the reason for his attraction to the wench? Because she was unattainable? Or because she struck a chord in him that he wanted her to unravel. Either way, the emotions he held for Selina were stronger than anything he had ever felt before, and he knew she felt the same.

"Nay."

"Then I think you know what you must do. If it is any consolation, I will offer my support in any way you need it."

"Thanks, lass."

Duncan stared into the fire, lost in his thoughts. He hadn't noticed Charlie curling into the pillows and pulling the quilt over herself. Nor did he when her eyes closed with a sigh. Even when her light snores whispered against the crackling logs, his thoughts consumed him. However, when he heard the room next to him open the door leading to the secret passage, he came out of his fog. He swore a string of curses, leaping from the chair, when he noted the sky changing to the colors of dawn. A light pink dotted the frayed distance of the midnight darkness. Soon, the servants would be about, and Charlie was still in his room.

"Wake up, Charlie. You must return to your room with haste." Duncan nudged Charlie on the shoulder.

"Mmm," Charlie moaned, swatting at Duncan.

Duncan growled at his dilemma. He scooped Charlie into his arms before he threw her over his shoulder. Still the lass slept. Charlie could sleep amongst the dead. He slipped through the corridor and it wasn't until he reached Charlie's bedroom before he heard her muffled curses whenever she banged against his backside. Duncan flipped Charlie onto her feet and covered her mouth.

"Hush. Now get in your room quick. It is almost dawn. You fell asleep on the settee. Sorry, love, for not waking you sooner."

Charlie dragged a hand through her hair, yawning. "'Tis not your fault."

"Get some more sleep. Thank you for your understanding ear." Duncan whispered, cupping her cheek tenderly and placing a kiss on her forehead.

Charlie smiled sleepily at Duncan, "Anytime."

Duncan gently pushed Charlie toward the opening before striding back into his room. He hoped that Evelyn slept as heavily as Charlie and didn't notice her sister's absence throughout the night. Either way, Charlie needed a husband and if Sinclair didn't step forward, then Duncan would protect Charlie from any scandal.

~~~~~

Sinclair pressed himself deeper into the shadows. When what he wanted to do most was to inject himself into the scene playing before him. The tender exchange between Charlie and Forrester twisted his heart into pieces. Her betrayal pierced his soul leaving behind an ache he doubted he could ever recover from. As much as wanted to look away he couldn't. Sinclair saw for himself the affection between the two. Charlie had reassured him that Forrester and she were only friends, and like a fool Sinclair had believed her. No, they were more than friends. Friends didn't visit each other in the cloak of darkness in secrecy. Nor did friends share a kiss, even one as innocent as on the forehead. No, these two shared a bond that would never break. Sinclair refused to share his wife with another man.

Once Forrester wandered back to his room, Sinclair stepped out of the shadows. He reached down to pick up the scrap of paper that had fallen out of Charlie's robe while Forrester carried her to her bedroom. Sinclair slipped the note into his pocket. He waited a few moments before he returned to his room. Sinclair dragged the chair near the window and propped his feet on the window seal. He reached over to grab the bottle of whiskey he'd confiscated from the duke's study. Lifting it to his lips, he drowned himself in his sorrows. Maybe, if he drank enough, the pain consuming him would sustain. After his first few swallows, he realized nothing could ever help him ease this ache. Only a kiss from her lips would. But that would only bring on another set of problems. He could never trust in her kiss again. No matter how sweet it was.

Sinclair dug into his pocket and unraveled the scrunched up note. He peered at the words: *Use the secret corridor and meet in my room at midnight.* While Sinclair had waited for Charlie to appear throughout the night she had already gifted herself to Forrester. Sinclair had spent the night pacing the corridor, fighting with himself at knocking at her bedroom door. Each time he talked himself into surprising her, he stopped. He would convince himself that if he knocked, he would be a selfish bastard in wanting to compromise her more than he already had. Then he would return to his room, defeated with himself. However, every time he twisted the ring around in his pocket, it would build his courage again to approach Charlie. He wanted to propose tonight. To secure her promise of a lifetime together.

After his fight with Worthington and Ralston over Charlotte in the village that evening, he'd realized that if he didn't propose, he could lose her. His reason wasn't because of the duke's offer. No, his reason stood because of the love he held for her. He didn't want to listen to another man speak Charlotte's name.

Sinclair had hoped that she would have come to him again. But after his conceited attitude at the picnic, Sinclair knew he'd riled Charlie's temper. And that he would need to be the one to make amends. Sinclair had only acted as he did, to draw attention off them. He noticed the duke's observation of them and her matchmaking aunt's not-so-subtle messages. When he dragged her into the woods, it was a moment of madness. When he re-emerged, her uncle had been on the way over to them. So when Charlie shoved him in the water, he taunted her some more to have the desired affect he achieved. When her uncle witnessed their exchange, he seemed pleased that Sinclair hadn't compromised her. Only the other gentlemen thought otherwise. They were furious after a few drinks at the tavern, and they let their displeasure show. Sinclair still felt a few twinges from where their fists landed. Gray and Forrester separated the fight, and they returned to the estate. Where Sinclair waited like the fool he was.

It was on the last talk he gave himself that he decided to risk everything for a moment of Charlie's time. Now the ring burned a hole in his pocket. A ring that upon tomorrow he would return to his mother's care. A ring that would never grace Charlotte's hand as he had planned.

Chapter Nineteen

Charlie's gaze searched the ballroom over Lord Worthington's shoulder for Jasper. He had made himself scarce throughout the day. When Charlie searched for him, she inquired to Lucas of his whereabouts. Lucas informed her that Jasper returned home to collect his mother for the ball. With a relief that he hadn't been avoiding her, Charlie took herself off to her bedroom to get ready for the ball. When she informed Evelyn of her doubts, she reassured Charlie that her imagination was getting the best of her. However, once the ball kicked into full swing, he still hadn't showed. After a few dances, Charlie's doubts resurfaced and left her wondering if the past few days were also a part of her imagination.

Once the dance ended, Worthington escorted Charlie back over to Evelyn's side. Her sister engaged Worthington in small talk to keep him there. Charlie slipped again into her search for Jasper. She found Lady Sinclair drinking a glass of champagne, talking to Aunt Susanna. Which meant Jasper was near. She wasn't mistaken when Jasper appeared by his mother's side returning from the dance floor with Gemma. Charlie's heart sped up at the sight of Jasper. She smoothed her trembling palms against her skirt. Jasper was strikingly handsome in his jet black greatcoat. The emerald waistcoat spanning his chest made her mouth water to what lay beneath. As her gaze traveled lower, she noticed his breeches fit him like a tight glove.

Every muscle outlined, leaving nothing to any lady's imagination. Charlie's gaze lifted to meet Jasper's eyes. His glare unsettled her.

"Would you give me the honor of the dinner dance?" Worthington asked Charlotte.

"Yes, yes of course," answered Charlie, distracted by Jasper. She didn't realize what she said yes to. She would say yes to anything to get Worthington to move on.

"Excellent. I shall return later this evening." Worthington said before he walked away.

"How could you?" Evelyn hissed before rushing away.

Oblivious to the conversation that just took place, Charlie tilted her head while keeping her gaze trained on Jasper. She didn't understand his misplaced anger. Why didn't he search her out when he arrived? Why didn't he come to her side now? Charlie's confusion only grew when he whispered something to his mother and turned to head in the opposite direction of Charlie.

When Charlie tilted her head at him, Jasper knew he had to put space between them quick. It would only be a matter of time before she came over to them. The carriage ride over was torture enough. His mother's constant questioning on who he had chosen for a bride grated on his nerves. He didn't have time to explain that he had changed his mind. That it was a foolish idea once he thought it through, and he'd decided he wasn't ready to settle down. Except a lame excuse wouldn't satisfy his mother. She would want details and wouldn't stop until she had them. Her interrogation would wear him down, and he didn't want to paint Charlie in such a scandalous picture. His mother and Charlie shared a close friendship that he wouldn't ruin. No matter how much Charlie had hurt him with her pursuits.

However, before Jasper could make his getaway, Charlie was upon them and greeting his mother. His mother pulled Charlie in for a hug and then held her back, gushing how amazing Charlie looked in her dress. Each compliment his mother paid toward Charlie only heightened the color on Charlie's cheeks. Her eyes glowed when they trailed over to him. His heart stopped in that moment, while his mouth dried up. His mother's praise didn't do Charlie justice. She was a vision before him, dressed in a buttercream creation made of silk and lace. Her hair lay in soft curls framing her face with a strand of pearls interwoven in the tresses. The only piece of jewelry she wore was a locket that had been a gift from her uncle when she first moved in. Charlie only ever wore the necklace on the most special of occasions. Jasper wondered what she kept hidden inside the locket. Something he would never know after tonight.

"Do you not think so, Jasper?"

"What do I think, Mother?"

"That Charlotte is the most striking lady at the ball this evening."

Charlie's cheeks turned the color of the reddest rose. Even with a blush, she was a sight to behold. That Jasper would never deny.

"You look very lovely this evening, Lady Holbrooke."

"Thank you, Lord Sinclair."

Lady Sinclair laughed. "Lord and lady. I have never known you two to be so proper." She held Charlotte's hands in hers, looking them over.

"I thought …" Lady Sinclair looked over at Jasper.

Jasper shook his head. "You were mistaken in your thoughts."

"I do not think so. What happened to the item you requested?"

"As I said, you were mistaken. I shall return the item to you on the morrow."

Charlie's head swiveled back and forth at the confusing conversation Jasper held with his mother. Lady Sinclair was adamant on the unspoken subject. With each of Jasper's denials, her fingers tightened around Charlotte's hand.

"What happened?" Lady Sinclair asked.

"Let us say that I was mistaken with my decision."

"Humph."

"If you ladies will excuse me." Sinclair made no excuse for his leave, because he had none. Only that he couldn't stay in the proximity of Charlie for another minute. Not without making both of them look like fools. He didn't allow the ladies time to respond before stalking away.

"I do not understand what has gotten into that boy. All day he prowled around the house in a state of doom. Then only became more agitated on the carriage ride over. Now he abandons us."

"You know Jasper, he hates these things." Charlie tried to make up an excuse for Jasper's behavior. However, it sounded false even to her ears.

"Yes, dear. That must be it. Now, will you please escort an old lady over to the other matrons? When your guests return home, you must pay me a visit to share the details of the house party. Promise?"

"I promise." Charlie smiled at Jasper's mother, making a promise to something she might not be able to keep.

After Charlotte settled Lady Sinclair next to Aunt Susanna, she went in search of Jasper. She wanted an explanation for his avoidance. His reaction toward Charlie confused her. One minute he devoured her with his eyes, then the next minute fury rolled off him. Charlie searched the house over and couldn't find him. She visited everywhere. Jasper wasn't in the card room, the billiard room, the library, or Uncle Theo's study. However, her uncle was there.

"Come in, Charlotte. I would like to have a few words with you. Please close the door."

Charlie nervously advanced to the desk. She sat down, perched on the edge of the chair. Ready to take flight at a moment's notice. Her uncle only smiled at her indulgently, so Charlie relaxed back in the chair. She worried he held knowledge of her activities. Instead, he paid compliments to her appearance and her behavior, *sans* the dunking of Lord Sinclair, during the house party. He continued declaring how proud of her he was, and he couldn't wait to show her off in London. Even promising to take her to Tattersall's to let her choose the livestock for their business venture. While his offer sounded amazing, it wasn't what her heart wished for, or what it expected. She had thought Sinclair would ask her to marry him and they would live happily ever after on his estate raising horses. A dream that seemed to be slipping away with each passing minute.

"Why the long face, my dear?"

"I am sorry, Uncle Theo. It all sounds wonderful. I guess I am a little tired from all the dancing."

"Yes, I noticed your dance card was quite full this evening. It reminded me of my sweet Olivia. All the gentlemen clamored for a chance to hold her in their arms. How I became so lucky to have made her mine, I am clueless even to this day."

"Because she loved you the first moment she laid on eyes on you."

"And I her," Uncle Theo sighed.

Charlie's lips lifted into a wistful smile. "I wish for the same."

"You have found it, my dear."

"I thought I had, only now I am not so sure."

"Nonsense."

"Then why does he avoid me?"

Uncle Theo laughed. "Because you scare him."

"Now you speak nonsense."

"Your gentleman has never had a vulnerable moment in his life. Every aspect has been given to him or he gained it easily. You, my dear, are a whirlwind he cannot control, nor will you make life easy and he knows that. Therefore his life will never be easygoing again and that scares him. He does not fear the love you have for one another, but the depth of what that emotion will do."

"We have not even spoken of love."

"Then there lies your problem, Charlie. Perhaps instead of waiting for the gentleman to confess his love, you need to confess your love first. Clear the doubts away."

"Do you know of which gentleman I speak of?"

"Yes, I am aware of which gentleman captured your heart."

"You will not force him, if he does not feel the same way?"

"No, but I will secure your future as I see fit, my dear."

Charlie nodded. She understood her uncle's underlying message. He may not force Sinclair to love her in return, but he would find her a groom soon. Charlie rose and placed a kiss on her uncle's cheek.

"I love you," she whispered on the verge of tears, rushing toward the door. This evening had been an emotional ride, leaving her confused for the future.

"Charlie?"

Charlie turned, swiping a tear from her cheek. "Yes?"

"I noticed Sinclair taking himself off to the stables."

"You did?"

"Yes."

Charlie beamed with excitement, her uncle's support made clear. Charlie threw the door open.

"At least change your dress," Uncle Theo yelled after Charlie.

Charlie rushed to her room, coming to a halt seeing Evelyn lying on the bed crying. She hurried to her sister's side, kneeling on the floor.

"What is wrong, dearest?"

"He asked you to supper, and you said yes."

"Who?"

"Worthington."

"No, you are mistaken."

"I stood next to you when he asked, and you answered yes." Evelyn cried harder.

Charlie closed her eyes, remembering that Worthington had asked her something, and she'd answered yes. She had grown irritated at his persistent company. Every time Charlie tried to direct him toward Evelyn, he only tried harder for Charlie's attention. In her annoyance, she had only given Worthington encouragement and hurt her sister.

"I have made such a mess. It was never my intention. I did not realize what he asked. My attention was focused on Jasper, and I only answered yes for him to leave me alone. I swear I had no clue to what he was asking."

"It no longer matters. I must face the fact that Worthington holds no interest in me."

"Nonsense. You must only try harder. Perhaps if you …" A knock sounded on the door, interrupting Charlie. .

Charlie rose and opened the door a crack, so as not to draw attention to Evelyn's distress state. Lucas stood agitated at the door, his hair standing on end and his cravat ripped open.

"Charlie, you must come quick. Sapphire is in labor and having a difficult time. Sinclair is with her now, but she needs your gentle attention."

"Wait for me to change."

"Hurry," Lucas shouted through the closed door.

Evelyn had heard Lucas and rose from the bed to help Charlie undress. After they discarded the many layers, Charlie slid into a pair of breeches and one of Lucas's old linen shirts. She stuffed her feet into boots and pulled a pair of work gloves from the wardrobe.

"I am sorry Evelyn, I must help Sapphire. Please promise that you will not give up on your hope for Worthington. If he is your true heart's desire, then you must fight for him."

Evelyn smiled through her tears. "I promise."

Charlie kissed Evelyn's cheek before she rushed out the door where Lucas waited. The two of them ran toward the servant staircase to sneak outside. While most of the guests knew of Charlie's eccentricity of dressing like a boy, it wasn't what they liked to parade about. Evelyn watched them from the window, running into the stables. Charlie wouldn't return for the rest of the evening.

Evelyn glanced over to Charlie's discarded dress. She knew in her heart that when Charlie told Worthington they could share the dinner dance, she hadn't meant it. Sinclair's absence had distracted her sister, and once he arrived that had been the only thing Charlotte obsessed over. Even though Charlie danced with Lord Worthington, her mind had been elsewhere.

No one would realize Charlie's absence at the ball. Her family wouldn't announce that Charlie was in the stable helping a horse give birth. To everyone, Charlie would spend the evening dancing and sharing a meal with Worthington. Nor would they notice Evelyn's disappearance. She had always been the quiet one who went unnoticed by all.

Evelyn started unbuttoning her dress and slipping off the bodice and skirt. Charlie would forgive Evelyn for the deception, and she only prayed Worthington would too. After she slipped on Charlie's dress and re-buttoned herself, she stood in the mirror and undid the ribbons in her hair. She brushed out her curls until they hung in waves, framing her face. If asked, she would say the pearls had fallen out of her hair. Once this evening finished, she promised herself that she would never pretend to be Charlie again. Evelyn only wanted one more night with Reese Worthington. In the morning, if she didn't hold a chance with him, then she would allow Uncle Theo to find a groom worthy of her love.

Chapter Twenty

Charlie crooned a lullaby to the foal suckling on her mother. Sapphire and her new baby made an amazing picture that Charlie wanted to stare at forever. Even though she gifted her uncle with Sapphire's first foal, she knew the horses would never be apart. What most didn't know was that Charlie owned Sapphire and Uncle Theo would never sell the foal. Perhaps he would even allow her to name the colt.

When she arrived at the stable and saw to Sapphire's comfort, all the tension with Jasper disappeared. Their only focus was on the horse's birthing. While Sapphire struggled toward the end, it was with their gentle care that the horse settled and delivered a beautiful golden baby. Charlie cried at the beautiful sight while laughing in delight. With a few more words of praise, Charlie slid out of the stall, leaving mama and baby some time alone. She moved to the next stall and settled down on a bed she made to stay close. The blanket was soft even though some hay poked through. However, her exhausted body didn't care. Charlie's eyes drifted shut even before her head hit the hay.

That was where Jasper found Charlie. He'd informed Gray he would make sure Charlie returned to the house protected. When Selina arrived in the middle of the birth shrieking her displeasure at his absence from the ball, Jasper assured Gray he would see to the birth and Charlie. Gray agreed reluctantly before returning to the house. Throughout the birth, Jasper's only focus had been on Sapphire. It was what happened after the birth that made Jasper want to run in the opposite direction. Charlie had thrown herself in his arms, thanking him for helping Sapphire. Before Charlie clung any tighter, Jasper stepped away from her. It was watching her stare at the mama and baby with tears in her eyes that made Jasper uncomfortable.

Charlie standing in the garments of a man with her hair styled like a lady was a sight to behold. However, it wasn't what she wore, but how she wore her heart on her sleeve. It was a look he wanted bestowed upon him for the rest of his life. However, for the first time in his life, Jasper wouldn't be selfish. He wouldn't trap Charlie into a marriage when her heart lay with another. When she sang to the horses, he listened to the soft melody melting his heart. After she finished, Jasper thought she would leave. Instead, she curled into a stall near the horses. Jasper couldn't leave her alone in the stable all night, and he knew Charlie wouldn't return to the house until morning.

Jasper closed his eyes and tilted his head back, blowing out a sigh. What he was about to do, would be foolish. But he wanted to hold her one more night before Forrester made an offer for her hand. Jasper lowered himself to the ground and drew Charlie into his arms. She moaned in her sleep and snuggled closer. Jasper's heart gave another tug. However, when Charlie murmured, "Love you, Jasper." Jasper's heart exploded. Jasper stilled, waiting for Charlie to say more. Instead, she only nuzzled her head into his chest and wrapped an arm around his middle. Jasper stared at the rafters, fighting the urge to awaken Charlie and to demand who her heart laid with. Soon he relaxed with Charlie and drifted to sleep.

Charlie shivered, snuggling deeper to find warmth. Her hand slid under the cover and encountered a warm, solid body. Charlie's eyes flashed open to find herself in Jasper's arms. His face relaxed in sleep with his mouth slightly open. Charlie never meant to wake him, but she couldn't stop herself from touching him. Her fingers lightly flickered across his cheek, along his neck. Her hand hovered over his chest, but instead of her hand she placed her lips on him. Pressing light kisses. When she raised her head, it was to find Jasper awake and watching her. Waiting for her next move.

With shaking fingers, Charlie undid the buttons on his shirt, spreading it open. She rolled over, straddling her body over his, her lips caressing his chest. She rose and lifted her shirt off over her head, laying herself bare to him.

"Charlie, stop."

"No."

"You will regret this come morning."

"How so?"

Charlie slid Jasper's shirt up to pull off. Her determination to rid him of his clothing didn't go unnoticed. Jasper meant to put a stop to it as soon as his arms were free, but when Charlie placed her lips on his, all rational intentions fled. Then when she pressed her breasts against his bare chest, he refused to resist her touch. Jasper pulled her head to his, devouring her mouth and sending the pearls in her hair scattering across the stall. He never answered her question.

Jasper slid his hand inside Charlie's loose breeches, brushing against her soft curls. When she arched into him, he sunk his fingers into her wetness, groaning at her readiness for him. He slid a finger inside her and Charlie bit his bottom lip. After he slid another finger inside, Charlie rocked her body on his hand. With one hand pleasuring her, the other hand gripped her head to his. Their tongues clashed with a need that only the other could fulfill. Jasper breathed his soul into Charlie with every kiss.

Charlie teetered on the verge of exploding with each stroke from Jasper. His kisses dominated her senses with each pull of his lips. She clung to him out of desperation. His odd behavior the last two days caused her to fear that she'd lost him. When Jasper lifted his head to draw a breath, Charlie pulled away and stood. With a hurry, she undid her trousers, dropping them to the ground. Charlie stood above Jasper, naked. His gaze devoured her, his eyes dipping to her breasts where they lingered while she drew in deep breaths, recovering from his onslaught of kisses. Then they lowered, scorching a path of desire with his gaze. His hands lingered on the back of her knees, tracing circles. Charlie's gaze lowered to his pants and noticed his hardness. Jasper still wanted her.

When Charlie stared at his cock like a starving woman, Jasper only hardened more. He needed this woman now. He would wait no longer to take her again. Jasper lifted his hips and stripped his pants off, throwing them against the wall. With a crook of his finger, he beckoned Charlie to lower herself on him.

Charlie knew what Jasper wanted and was more than happy to oblige him. She wanted Jasper to answer her question, but she needed him inside her more than an explanation. Charlie lowered herself with her knees straddling Jasper. Jasper stroked his cock before he guided it inside Charlie. Charlie's eyes widened at the pressure. With one hand on Jasper's chest, Charlie wiggled lower, taking him deeper.

It took everything Jasper had to stay still. If he moved, he would explode inside Charlie without a single stroke. Charlie may have been wet with need, but her pussy gripped his cock tight. When she rotated her hips in small circles, he grasped her hips holding on. With each movement, Jasper realized Charlie gained confidence in pleasing him. Each time she rose and slid him back inside her, his groans echoed around him. Her pace quickened with a smile of a siren gracing her face at the power she held.

Charlie took Jasper inside her deeply, lighting a fire around them with each stroke. Their passion built a need so deep, Charlie didn't know if they would ever fulfill it. Each time she rocked her body with Jasper's, his eyes clouded with a possessive desire. She got so lost in the depths, she hadn't realized when each time she lowered herself onto him, he would push his hips into hers. Their strokes rose into a rising inferno of need. Jasper pulled Charlie into him, claiming her mouth while he claimed her body. Charlie clung to him, and Jasper inhaled her cry of pleasure.

Their bodies shook from their passion exploding. Jasper lay back, pulling Charlotte with him. She rested on his chest, catching her breath. Jasper's hold only tightened the longer they were together. He was a selfish bastard for what he just did, and now he didn't want to let Charlie go.

Charlie pressed a kiss on Jasper's chest. "Jasper, while I love lying in your arms, I must breathe."

Jasper dropped his arms to his sides. Before Charlie moved, he rolled out from underneath her. Jasper jumped to his feet, searching for his clothes. He found his breeches and stepped into them and pulled his shirt over his head. All the while Charlie lay there naked. After he stood there dressed and raking his hand through his hair, she pulled the blanket over herself.

"I only needed to breathe, there was no rush for you to dress."

"This was a mistake. I took advantage of you."

Charlie grinned cheekily at Jasper. "Mmm. Are you sure I did not take advantage of you?" Charlie jumped up, wrapping the blanket around them.

Jasper pulled away. "Charlie, for Christ's sake, put your clothes back on."

Charlie backed farther away. Jasper looked at Charlie with disgust. Only a few moments ago, his stare held desire, passion, and even love. Now he seemed repulsed by her. Charlie got dressed with as much dignity that she could muster. She now understood that while Jasper enjoyed the use of her body, it was where their relationship ended. When Charlie tried to brush past him in her hurry to leave, Jasper grabbed her arm. A shiver ran down her spine. How could something so pleasant also hold displeasure?

"Let me go."

Jasper dropped his hand, "We must talk."

Charlie turned toward him with her chin held high. The only emotion betraying her were the tears forming in her eyes. "We have nothing more to discuss, Lord Sinclair."

"You may feel that way. However, I want you to understand that I will not interfere with Forrester's pursuit."

Charlie gasped. "You have knowledge of Duncan's pursuit?"

"Yes, I held suspicion and I will get my jealousy under control."

"You are jealous?"

"How else should I feel? Explain to me how I can live in this state of turbulent emotion."

"I never realized you held such strong emotions."

"Have I not bared my soul every time we have made love?"

"But you never spoke the words."

"And neither have you."

"I love you, Jasper."

"You are very free with your love, Charlie. I find those words do not hold the same meaning as mine do."

"And what are your words, Jasper?"

"You are the very air that fills the heart of my soul."

"Oh." Charlie had never heard anything so romantic. The only flaw was her confusion. She didn't understand if Jasper was professing his undying love or letting her go.

"Jasper?"

"Yes."

"I am quite confused."

"I can understand with your inexperience how that would be so. This week has been very eventful for a girl who has never received attention from a gentleman before. I lay the blame at my feet for my ardent pursuit of your affections."

"Which I have freely given to you."

"Yes, but you do not understand how your actions have confused other gentlemen. When a lady gives her favors to one gentleman, she should not give them so freely to others."

"Yet my confusion grows even more." Charlie stood perplexed at Jasper's conversation.

"I saw Forrester return you to your room last night."

Charlie nodded, beginning to understand how Sinclair might have misinterpreted what he witnessed.

"Do you promise not to tell a soul of Duncan's pursuit?"

"Charlie, by what honor I have remaining I cannot allow you to keep this a secret from your uncle. I will stand to the side, only if Forrester makes an offer for your hand."

"Why would Duncan make an offer for my hand? I presumed that would be an act you would attempt."

"Charlie, stop with the act. I know of your affair with Forrester."

Now it all made sense. Jasper had no clue about Duncan's infatuation with Selina Pemberton. Jasper thought Duncan wanted Charlie. How absurd.

Charlie would have doubled over laughing at the irony, if Jasper didn't stand before her wearing such a tortuous expression.

"Jasper, Duncan and I are only friends. I have explained this to you already."

"And friends do not visit each other in the secrecy of night. Nor do they share tender expressions with one another."

"They do if they love each other as family. I visited Duncan's room because he needed my advice on a lady he wishes to pursue. Nothing more."

"I know what I saw. He cares for you."

"As a sister. He loves another lady. A love that will only end badly in his case."

"Why?"

"It is not my story to share. I cannot betray Duncan's secret."

"So, you might have more late-night trysts with him whenever he needs you?"

"Perhaps."

"Exactly."

"Exactly what, Sinclair? Exactly, you hold no trust in me. Exactly, you think I am a trollop who shares my body willingly to any man that pays me attention. Exactly the ultimate truth of the matter, you do not believe in my love. You, my lord, are exactly a fool."

Charlie stormed past Jasper, stomping out of the stable. The man was as infuriating as ever. Why she opened her heart to such a brute was beyond her. At every turn she'd trusted him, only for him to think the worst of her. And to think, Charlie thought he would ask her to marry him. It would appear she was the fool. A fool in love with a condescending arse.

Jasper stood staring at the spot Charlie had just left. The accuracy of her words settled in his brain to make sense. He was a fool who ruined an amazing lady he loved with his false accusations. Now that he remembered all the times Charlie interacted with Forrester, and it was with the same regard she showed Gray. Amusement lit her eyes when Forrester flirted outrageously with her. Never love.

When Jasper shook himself from his stupor, he tore off after Charlie. He expected to have to search through the house and cause a scene to find her. Instead, when he flew out of the stable, it was to find her waiting for him with her arms crossed and her foot tapping in agitation. He smiled. This he could handle. His spitfire raging mad. He would endure whatever tirade she spouted. In the end he would humble himself at her feet with his own apology and beg for forgiveness. Then for her love for an eternity.

"You, Jasper Sinclair, have nothing but air in between your ears. You insult me with your idiocy. Then you reject my love because of a fool's imagination. You have broken my heart with *your* insensitive heart. I shall now have to spend the rest of my life wondering how I could have fallen in love with such a buffoon. Not only that, please tell me how I am to explain to *my* children that their father has no common sense."

Jasper smiled widely, falling even more in love with Charlotte. "There is no need to be so harsh, my love. My only excuse is that I have been so blinded by your love that I could not see the truth before my eyes. We shall explain to *our* children that the love I hold for their mother makes me foolish with happiness."

"I love you, Jasper, you fool."

"And I love you, Charlotte, my wild hoyden."

"I have not forgiven you yet. I expect complete groveling over the course of the next few days."

"Of course, my dear." Jasper pulled Charlie into his arms, smiling down at her.

"You can kiss me now," Charlie demanded.

"With pleasure."

After a few kisses coaxing Charlie's anger away, she soon sighed in his arms. Her lips grew softer under his. When her body melted against him, Jasper felt a sense of relief settle over them.

"I am truly sorry, my love. My jealousy consumed me at all the attention paid your way. From Forrester, to Worthington, to Ralston. I allowed the complex emotion to come between us."

"For no need, because I did not enjoy the extra attention I received. However, it could not be helped with the offer my uncle dangled before each of you gentleman if they won my hand."

Jasper drew back, surprised. "You knew?"

Charlie laughed. "Yes. Not at first, but when Aunt Susanna dropped a hint about Uncle Theo meeting with you gentlemen, it did not take long to find out what the stakes were."

"I am not accepting the foal."

"Yes, you are. You won the deal. Unless you do not plan on asking for my hand. In that case ..."

"There is no other case. If you would be patient, I wanted to ask you in a romantic setting."

"I do not need that nonsense."

Jasper sighed, dropping his arms. With Charlie's impatience for everything to happen in life at once, Jasper would never grow bored. If he ever wanted to surprise Charlie, he would have to plan ahead and make it appear spontaneous. He slipped his hand inside his pocket and pulled out the ring. He lifted Charlie's hand and slid the ring down her finger.

"Charlie, my love, will you do me the honor of becoming my bride?"

Charlie tilted her head and smiled, making him wait. Her smile only grew the longer she kept him waiting.

"I am not so sure. I will get back with you."

Jasper growled and lifted her over his shoulder, stomping back inside the stable. He dropped her into the hay and called her everything from a minx to a siren as he discarded his clothing. Charlie slipped off her clothes, her face glowing with desire. When Jasper claimed her, Charlie sighed her answer of yes into his kiss. Her answer sealed their fate that night.

Chapter Twenty-One

Charlotte descended the stairs, eager to join Jasper in his meeting with Uncle Theo. He'd promised to wait for her to share their news. She had hoped to tell Evelyn first when she returned to their bedroom in the early morning, but her sister wasn't there. Also, Evelyn didn't sleep in her bed last night. Which wasn't unusual, since they sometimes slept with Jacqueline in her bedroom. Something they had done since they were children. Charlotte rounded the staircase railing and stopped when she saw Evelyn with her ear pressed to the study door. When Charlie drew closer, she heard the raised voices. Evelyn raised her head once she noticed Charlotte.

"I am so sorry, Charlie."

"For what?"

"I never intended …"

"Like hell you did." Charlie heard Jasper roar before a scuffle broke loose.

Charlie threw the door open to see Jasper holding Worthington by his cravat with his arm cocked back, ready to throw a punch. Another punch, from the redness already staining Worthington's face. A sinking weight settled in the pit of Charlie's stomach when she pieced together why Jasper wanted to kill Worthington. With a swift glance at Evelyn, she understood the layout of the puzzle. The few remaining scattered pieces would cause a mismatched picture if not properly placed.

"Charlotte, please inform your uncle of your promise for our union," Worthington addressed Evelyn.

Evelyn stood in shock that Worthington stared at her, but addressed her as Charlotte. Everyone stood in the room waiting for Evelyn to speak, but no words came out. Charlotte's heart twisted for her sister. Charlie walked to Jasper's side, releasing his grip on Worthington and pulling him away. She slid her palm into Jasper's and squeezed. Jasper returned the squeeze, understanding the mistake and offering her support.

Worthington straightened his clothing, smoothing his hair back into place. He offered Evelyn a smile. Before he approached her side, the duke spoke out.

"Evelyn, if you will please close the door. Our family needs to have a private conversation that the rest of the house party need not be privy too. I assume the gentlemen in this room also see the need for secrecy in protecting Charlotte and your reputation."

Still Evelyn didn't move from her spot. She stood frozen, realizing the implications of her actions would now be revealed. Evelyn looked to her sister with fear. She had used Charlie's name to ruin herself for what she thought was love. Only she wasn't certain of what emotion she felt. Evelyn noticed the love shining from her sister's eyes, and Jasper returned the same love toward Charlie. He held Charlotte's hand in support, while the man she loved held himself aloof. Worthington only wanted Evelyn to confess to her promise because of a stupid horse. While he might look at her with desire and kiss with a passion neither of them could deny, it still didn't take away from the fact that he didn't realize who she was. He'd assumed she was Charlie, because that was who Evelyn duped him to believe. Evelyn was a fool to think she could change a man like Worthington's mind. She would never excite Worthington.

"I will close the door, Father. Evelyn and Charlotte, if you will please take a seat. Then we shall clear the confusion," said Lucas.

However, before Lucas reached it, Evelyn spun on her heel and shut the door quietly. Then, with her head held high, she sat on the settee. Charlie joined her and wrapped her arm around Evelyn's shoulders. Evelyn saw Worthington's confusion grow.

Uncle Theo rose from behind his desk and moved in front of the fireplace. He took stock of the room, forming his opinions on how one of his nieces had two gentlemen fighting for her hand. Some would say—his son especially—that inviting the selected gentlemen to his house party would end in a scandal. While both nieces engaged in scandalous courtships, they did so out of love. However, only one of them found love and happiness. The other must fight for it. A challenge his niece needed to attempt to experience the emotion of life. She had lived in her shell long enough. And if her determination from a few moments ago was any indication, she had realized it too.

"Very well, since Lord Worthington requested an audience first, before Lord Sinclair so crudely interrupted us, he shall speak first. Lord Worthington?"

Lord Worthington stepped forward, addressing the duke. "As I was saying, my courtship with your niece has been unorthodox and I apologize for overstepping my bounds with her virtue. My only excuse is that I am smitten."

"How were you smitten?" asked the duke.

"Why with her charm."

"What do you find charming about my niece?"

"Does it matter? The deed has already been done. I am only asking for your blessing, not your permission," Worthington said, agitated.

All eyes were upon him with each a different expression. Not that he realized the attention. His only focus was on the Duke of Colebourne. Worthington didn't care what anyone thought. He only cared about the duke's reaction.

"This deed you speak of, will there be consequences from them?"

"There is a possibility."

"I demand to know when this took place."

Worthington winced, "After the dinner dance."

"Then you are pledging your honor that you will protect my niece by marrying her?"

"Yes. That was your goal all along, was it not?" Worthington sneered.

"It was."

"Then I pledge my honor. Plan the wedding. When I return to collect the foal, I will collect my bride."

"The foal is not yours to collect," Jasper snarled.

Worthington laughed. "I am afraid so, Sinclair. I warned you the other evening that I would stop at nothing to make Charlotte mine. After I took her to my bed last night, there is no longer any hope for you to hold onto."

"Oh *no*. Evelyn, what have you done?" Charlie whispered.

Charlie's whisper echoed in the silent room, drawing everyone's notice their way. Through it all, Evelyn sat poised. She mouthed her apology to Charlie. The only trace of Evelyn's despair was the sadness in her eyes. The gentleman who ruined Evelyn didn't even know her.

"What did you two do?" asked Lucas.

"They have taken it upon themselves to seek happiness. While they deceived us by switching identities, they did not do so out of spite. Am I correct?" asked Uncle Theo.

"Yes," Charlotte and Evelyn answered.

Uncle Theo nodded before turning toward Sinclair, "Lord Sinclair, you may speak your request now."

"Mine is the same as Worthington's. Not permission, but a blessing. I asked Charlie to become my bride, and she has accepted. I, too, took your niece's innocence. However, the love I hold for Charlotte is unexplainable. She is the sunshine to my day and the moon to my night. And I want to explore every day with her for years to come."

Uncle Theo's smile beamed at Sinclair's declaration. "Blessing given. I have waited patiently enough for you both to realize it. I can tell by my niece's expression that the feeling is mutual."

Worthington said, "Your niece plays favor with two gentlemen and you are approving? What madness is this? I requested Charlotte's hand first."

"No, Lord Worthington, you did not. You requested my niece's hand, and you did not specify which niece. I assumed you meant Evelyn, since she is the niece you have ruined, not Charlotte."

"Nonsense, Charlotte wore the cream-colored gown at the ball. I could not even tell you the shade of Evelyn's gown because I do not focus my attention on dull debutantes. I requested Charlotte's hand for the dinner dance, and the niece I ate dinner and snuck away with was Charlotte.

"Did you sneak away to the stables?"

"No," Worthington answered in disgust. "I may love horses, but I hold more respect for a lady than to ruin her in such a location."

"Then you are unaware of the birth of Sapphire's foal?"

"When?"

"Last night when you were ruining my niece."

"I am sorry, Charlotte. I know how much you wanted to witness the birth." Worthington once again addressed Evelyn.

"Worthington," Lucas growled.

"What?"

"You cannot even tell them apart. What in the hell have you done?" Lucas advanced on Worthington.

"Enough." Evelyn stood. "Lord Worthington, I must confess. Charlotte and I have been switching places. The blame does not lie with her, but with me. I convinced her to deceive you when I realized you were to be a guest. A deceit I now regret to have taken, because of the consequences involved. Please accept my apologies for playing you the fool. It was I who you made lo … had sexual congress with."

"What?" roared Worthington. "Do you realize the implications of your treachery? You have ruined me. I needed that horse, it was the only reason I slept with you. Why I paid court to you or your sister. I do not even know any more. My pay day was to become Charlotte's husband so I could own the foal."

Charlotte watched her sister break into a million pieces at Worthington's declaration. Evelyn's skin paled, but she bit her lower lip from expressing her distress. But still Charlotte watched Evelyn's body shake. From hurt or anger, Charlotte didn't know.

"I am truly sorry, my lord."

"Sorry?" Worthington snapped. "You owe me a horse, Colebourne. Since Sinclair won the foal, you are going to sell me Sapphire for your niece's duplicity."

"Sapphire is not mine to sell," said Colebourne.

"Gray?"

Lucas shook his head.

"She is mine." Charlie stood.

"What?" Both Sinclair and Worthington asked.

Charlie nodded.

Sinclair started laughing. Of course, his love owned the horse. He should have known. All the signs were there. The duke had never even shown interest in Sapphire, leaving Charlie to make all the decisions for the animal. At first it frustrated Sinclair, then he grew to admire Charlie's talent when dealing with the temperamental horse. Charlie beamed at him, and Sinclair pulled her to him and kissed her in front of her family. Life with Charlie would never be boring.

"Then the foal you dangled in our faces was not yours to give," Worthington said.

"It was mine. Charlie promised Sapphire's first born to me," Colebourne answered.

Worthington looked at them with disgust before he turned to stride toward the door.

"Lord Worthington, where are you going?"

"I am returning to my estate and escaping this madness."

"I shall have Evelyn pack her bags."

Worthington turned, "Whatever for?"

"You made a promise to marry my niece."

"Your niece deceived me."

"Yes, she did. However, it does not take away your actions or your promise. Since I wish for no scandal to ensue, and I am sure you wish the same, considering your current circumstances, a swift ride to Gretna Green will solve this particular problem. Or else you can return to your current state of affairs before this house party began."

"You leave me no choice in the matter. I leave here not gaining a horse, but a bride. Could I ask for anything more?"

"You could, but I see no reason you would need to. Evelyn is worth so much more than a simple horse. One day you will realize that. I only hope for your sake it is not too late."

Worthington didn't answer the duke. He turned toward Evelyn. "I will give you two hours to pack and to say your goodbyes. I will make the arrangements for our travels." With a bow, he left the study.

Jasper whispered to Charlie that he would meet her later. Lucas left to inform Jacqueline, Gemma, and Abigail to meet in the twin's bedroom. They remained with Uncle Theo, whose smile was mixed with happiness and a twist of sadness.

"I wish your parents were alive to be here."

"We are sorry, Uncle Theo," Charlie said.

"Why? Life has not been so exciting for such a long time."

"You are not mad?" asked Evelyn.

"No. However, I will be if you do not bring that man around."

"It is hopeless. He does not love me. Hell, he still confuses me with Charlotte."

"Evelyn! Such language," said Charlie.

Uncle Theo laughed. "Worthington will be a challenge, but one that you need. It is time for you to live again, my dear. It will not be easy, but love never is. I will miss both of you in my life every day, but I look forward to your little miniature versions running around soon. Now off to your room, you have bags to pack."

Charlotte and Evelyn wrapped their arms around Uncle Theo for a hug, and they both kissed him on the cheek like they did when they were young. He never judged them and always accepted them for who they were, even when they disappointed him. However, he never let his disappointment rule the love he held for them.

When they reached their room, it was to find Jacqueline, Gemma, and Abigail waiting with Lucas. They were crying and laughing their enjoyment at the wonderful news. Lucas spun a tale of Evelyn and Worthington's courtship. He hid the cruelty of Worthington's words from the rest of the family. Evelyn's marriage to him would be hard enough without having the wrath of her family fighting against them. After Lucas spoke a few quiet words to Evelyn, he departed, but not before sharing a lingering glance with Abigail.

Once they'd packed Evelyn's chest and the footmen carried it, she hugged her family goodbye, promising to write once she arrived at her new home. After everyone left, Evelyn hugged Charlie, hanging on tightly.

"Will you ever forgive me for wearing your dress after you left?"

"There is nothing to forgive. If our situation were reversed, I would have done the same. Are you certain you want to marry Worthington? You can change your mind. Say the word. Jasper and I will hide you until the scandal passes."

"No. Jasper and you are going to start your marriage with happiness, not dread. I have made my bed, now I must lie in it."

"A cold one. Worthington gives me the shivers."

"Then I will have to warm it up, will I not?" Evelyn arched her brow.

Charlie laughed. Evelyn had come into herself this last week. A wicked self at that. Perhaps she should feel sorry for Worthington instead. The look in Evelyn's eyes gave Charlotte the chills.

"I love you, sis."

"I love you, Charlotte. Now, write to me all the details of your lovely wedding. I wish I could be here, but I know I cannot. So I want to hear all the delicious details later. Promise?"

"Promise."

~~~~~~

Jasper stood by Charlie's side, watching the carriage carrying Worthington and Evelyn depart along the long driveway. His own happiness didn't keep Jasper from holding pity for Worthington. Jasper saw the determination in Evelyn's eyes at Worthington's disregard and knew that if she was anything like her sister, Worthington didn't stand a chance. Charlie sniffed at his side. He looked down at his love and knew losing her sister under these circumstances would put a damper on their own plans.

After the rest of the family scattered away, Jasper guided Charlie toward her favorite tree. The one place Charlie always felt safe from changes. He sat against the tree trunk and held his hand out for her to sit. She lowered herself and Jasper settled Charlie in between his legs and pulled her back against his chest. They sat there silently, letting the peacefulness of the scenery quiet their thoughts. From time to time Jasper would place soft kisses on the top of Charlie's head.

"Will they find happiness?" Charlie asked.

"Yes. I believe they will."

"So do I."

"Since I got the girl, and she owns the horse, maybe we can gift the foal to Worthington."

"For a wedding present?"

"Yes."

Charlie squealed, turning in his arms. "That is a wonderful idea, my love. You are an amazing generous man."

"Would you like me to show you how amazing?" Jasper placed a kiss on Charlie's neck.

"Mmm. I would, but I do not think Uncle Theo and your mother watching from the veranda would care to see," Charlie teased.

Jasper looked up to find the Duke of Colebourne and his mother staring fondly at them. He rose quickly, dumping Charlie on the ground. At Charlie's laughter, he dragged her up and then stood a respectable distance away.

"You are a devilish minx," Jasper growled.

"And you are a devilish rake."

"Shall we share our news with my mother?" Jasper offered his arm.

"Only if you promise to visit me in my room after everyone retires for the evening to show me how amazing. I will be so lonely sleeping by myself." Charlie pouted.

"Not for long, my dear. Before the month is out, you will be mine."

"Must we wait that long?"

"Yes, it will draw the scandal away from Evelyn. Also, Mother will never forgive us if we do not marry in the village church."

"Then let us tell her quick. So we can plan a wedding. I am eager to become Lady Sinclair."

Jasper stopped and kissed Charlotte, soft and slow. He didn't care who saw them. He only cared that he held Charlotte in his arms. Her kisses were a fuel to the fire of her soul. However, if he didn't stop, they would have more to explain away to her uncle and his mother. With a laugh, he pulled away. Charlie tilted her head and then joined in with his laughter.

Epilogue

Jasper watched his wife stroke the foal and talk softly. Only it was more for her comfort than for Cobalt. Even though they'd decided to give the colt to Worthington and Evelyn for a wedding present, Jasper knew Charlie would miss Sapphire's first offspring. Just as she missed her sister. Jasper decided now was the time to surprise Charlie with his news.

"Good morning, love."

"Morning, Jasper. Sorry I rose early. I wanted to say goodbye to Cobalt one last time."

"That is a relief."

"What is a relief?"

"As I ate breakfast in bed alone, I began to have doubts that you no longer enjoyed our marital bed considering how early you rose and how fast you fell asleep last night."

Charlie blushed. "You know darn well why I fell asleep last night. 'Twas almost dawn before we … well, you know." Charlie's hand fluttered in the air.

Jasper advanced on her with the same determination he held in bed during the night. His desire was never satisfied with a simple kiss. No, Jasper had to consume Charlie with his overpowering love. Her husband still left her in a state of muddled confusion every time he glanced her way. With every caress. With every kiss upon her lips.

"Before we finished making love?" Jasper asked, stealing a kiss from Charlie.

"Mmm." Charlie moaned.

"Before you distract me again with your uncontrollable passion, I have a surprise for you."

"My uncontrollable passion? Why, my lord … You have a surprise?"

"My, how one can get distracted from an adoring husband for a surprise," Jasper teased.

"Perhaps, if said husband stops with his tormenting, his wife would adore him again."

"Mmm, you do not say?"

"Spill the surprise, Sinclair."

"How would you like to travel with Cobalt to Worthington's estate on our way to London? Perhaps stay a few days and visit with Evelyn."

Charlie shouted her excitement, jumping on Jasper. She wrapped her legs around his waist and her arms around his neck. She showered kisses all over his face with her pleasure. Then she took his lips under hers and kissed her love for him. Each kiss built their passion to a level of uncontrollable desire. Charlie still didn't understand how they ignored what was always before their eyes. It no longer mattered, because every day they basked in the glory of the love they discovered.

"Is that a yes?"

"Yes, my adoring husband. Now if you are finished with your teasing, I shall show you how much I adore you."

Charlie didn't give Jasper time to tease her again, before her lips descended to his neck and her fingers made quick work to unbutton his shirt. Jasper groaned and backed them into an empty stall. He sunk them down onto the blanket and pillows that he kept for this very purpose.

They spent the morning showing how much they adored each other with every caress and kiss. Each time they made love it was a discovery into the depth of their love for one another. There was nothing more perfect for them than making love slowly, then holding each other whispering of their plans for the future. While most of their time they spent loving each other, there were the few times when their tempers exploded around them. Which only made their love-making explosive when they made up. Life spent as Lord and Lady Sinclair was never boring, but an adventure to enjoy for years to come.

Look for Evelyn & Reese's story in early 2021!

If you would like to hear my latest news then visit my website www.lauraabarnes.com to join my mailing list.

"Thank you for reading How the Lady Charmed the Marquess. Gaining exposure as an independent author relies mostly on word-of-mouth, so if you have the time and inclination, please consider leaving a short review wherever you can."

Author Laura A. Barnes

International selling author Laura A. Barnes fell in love with writing in the second grade. After her first creative writing assignment, she knew what she wanted to become. Many years went by with Laura filling her head full of story ideas and some funny fish songs she wrote while fishing with her family. Thirty-seven years later, she made her dreams a reality. With her debut novel *Rescued By the Captain*, she has set out on the path she always dreamed about.

When not writing, Laura can be found devouring her favorite romance books. Laura is married to her own Prince Charming (who for some reason or another thinks the heroes in her books are about him) and they have three wonderful children and two sweet grandbabies. Besides her love of reading and writing, Laura loves to travel. With her passport stamped in England, Scotland, and Ireland; she hopes to add more countries to her list soon.

While Laura isn't very good on the social media front, she loves to hear from her readers. You can find her on the following platforms:

You can visit her at *www.lauraabarnes.com* to join her mailing list.

Website: **http://www.lauraabarnes.com**
Amazon: **https://amazon.com/author/lauraabarnes**
Goodreads: **https://www.goodreads.com/author/show/16332844.Laura_A_Barnes**
Facebook: **https://www.facebook.com/AuthorLauraA.Barnes/**
Instagram: **https://www.instagram.com/labarnesauthor/**
Twitter: **https://twitter.com/labarnesauthor**
BookBub: **https://www.bookbub.com/profile/laura-a-barnes**

Desire more books to read by Laura A. Barnes
Enjoy these other historical romances:

Matchmaking Madness Series:
How the Lady Charmed the Marquess

Tricking the Scoundrels Series:
Whom Shall I Kiss… An Earl, A Marquess, or A Duke?
Whom Shall I Marry… An Earl or A Duke?
I Shall Love the Earl
The Scoundrel's Wager
The Forgiven Scoundrel

Romancing the Spies Series:
Rescued By the Captain
Rescued By the Spy
Rescued By the Scot

Printed in Great Britain
by Amazon